Shadows

Joan De La Haye

F✦X SPIRIT

www.foxspirit.co.uk

A Fox Spirit Original Novel
Fox Spirit Books
www.foxspirit.co.uk
adele@foxspirit.co.uk

ISBN: 978-0-9573297-7-5

Cover art by Dave Johnson

Layout by Vincent Holland-Keen
http://www.vincenthollandkeen.co.uk/

typesetting and ebook conversion by handebooks.co.uk

Third Edition August 2012

Distributed by Fox Spirit

Acknowledgement

Jayne Southern, my fabulous editor, for her neverending patience and fabulous sense of humour.

Anina and Jacques Stenvert, wonderful friends.

Laura and Justin for all your love and support and reading all my short stories.

Laurence Cramer, for all the crits, advice and drinking till dawn. The bottles of Grants were worth it!

Thanks Mom – for everything!

Johan and Eileen, the best siblings a girl could ask for.

1

The lights from the Seven Eleven reflected in puddles of murky rainwater. At eleven o'clock at night, the parking area was deserted. Kevin stepped inside the store in search of something to eat while I waited in the car for him.

My father's funeral had been that morning, and Kevin thought a night out would be the best way to take my mind off how he'd died. It hadn't helped. All I could think about was that I hadn't been able to say good-bye or tell him that I loved him. I couldn't even get drunk and forget about it, I couldn't pretend that I was okay and put on a happy face for the sake of Kevin and his friends. As a result we cut the night short, which irritated Kevin's friends and I was once again the party pooper.

Kevin had been gone for what seemed like a few seconds when everything that I knew and trusted in my life changed forever.

I was rudely distracted from my reverie by an annoying tapping on my window. I was about to hurl off a few choice words at the offending party, until I saw his face. My stomach churned, my self-pity party transformed into a Stephen King novel.

Yellow eyes stared back at me. Sharp, pointed teeth, filed into fangs, snarled. He shook my door handle. My heart rate jumped sky high. He was gone as fast as he'd appeared.

I took a deep breath and looked around. No sign of him. I took another deep breath and breathed out slowly.

"What the hell was that?" I stammered.

I managed to get my heart rate down, but couldn't quite get the hair on the back of my neck to go back to normal. My skin wouldn't stop crawling. Goose bumps appeared on my skin and the smell of sulphur wafted up my nostrils.

Something scraped the driver's side of the car. I hoped it was Kevin returning with a strong drink: preferably a bottle of tequila. I turned to look and my heart sank. The scary-looking man with fangs was back. Kevin had left the car unlocked. Panic gripped my palpitating heart. Who didn't lock their car in Johannesburg? He shook the door. I leaned over the driver's seat and slammed the lock down. The central locking did its job. Then he was gone again.

"Breathe, just breathe." I repeated it over and over again, while I doubled over and put my head between my knees. I squeezed my eyes shut. He was playing games with me and I didn't know the rules. I felt helpless. I wanted to scream, but fear had a stranglehold on my throat, silencing me.

Tap tap.

I plugged my ears with my fingers. It wasn't happening.

Tap tap.

Turning my head to the left, I opened one eye.

Glass shattered.

I screamed.

He pulled my hair.

"Oh, God. Oh, God," I moaned. I was about to be raped and murdered while I waited for Kevin to come out of the Seven Eleven.

"Babe, are you okay?" Kevin sat in the driver's seat next to me, with a worried expression on his face. "You were groaning."

I looked around in shock. There was no sign of broken glass anywhere. All the windows were intact.

"Are you alright?" Kevin asked again.

"I'm fine."

"You look like you've seen a ghost."

"I'm fine." I wasn't sure if what I'd seen had been real or imagined, but Kevin obviously wasn't going to let it go. Not sure what to tell him, I decided to tell him a version of the truth.

"Some drunk guy was messing around with me and gave me a bit of a fright. That's all." I didn't want Kevin to think I'd inherited my father's mental problems. According to my sister, my father had been rather irrational before his death. I thought it was more along the lines of being completely loony tunes. I was relieved that I hadn't been around to see him like that. At least I remembered him the way he was before our estrangement.

"Maybe we should call the cops or something?"

"What for?"

"I don't know. Maybe to arrest him for being drunk and disorderly, or something."

"Oh please. Like the cops are really going to give a damn about some guy banging on a girl's window and giving her a fright. They've got bigger fish to fry."

I wanted to get out of there; the thought of hanging out in the parking lot a few hours for the cops to show up didn't appeal to me in the slightest.

"This is true."

"Besides I just want to go home and forget about everything." I breathed out and took another deep breath. "I just want to curl up in your arms."

"Now that's a very good idea."

"I thought you might think so."

I let go of the breath I was holding, once I saw the deserted shopping complex slide by in the side view mirror. But no matter how hard I tried, I couldn't shake the feeling that someone was watching me. Rain started drizzling down as we drove away. Neon signs shimmered in the puddles.

*

The drive home was uneventful. A feeling stirred in my gut that wouldn't go away. I ground my teeth and hoped that a night clinging to Kevin would drive out those dark shadows lurking in my mind.

The electric gate screamed for more oil as it opened. I gripped Kevin's leg a little harder than I'd intended. He winced from the pain, quickly removed my hand from his thigh, but held it tightly as we drove up the driveway. It was reassuring having him hold my hand like that. His touch made me feel safe. The gate slammed shut behind us.

"Are you sure you're okay?" Kevin asked, not looking at me. "What with your dad and now that guy...." His fingers tapped on the steering wheel. He wasn't very good with handling people who were a little upset. He liked it when things were nice and normal. As long as everything seemed to be smooth on the surface, he was happy. We came to a stop at the back of the main house and in front of my one-bed-roomed cottage.

"I'm fine." I got out of the car and closed the door a touch too hard.

"Hey, my car didn't do anything to you."

He loved his car. He spent hours primping and polishing it. His car was cleaner than he was most of the time. Sometimes I had the feeling that his car was more important than I was.

"I'm sorry, the handle slipped out of my hand."

He shook his head and locked the car with the remote and walked me to the door in silence. My hands shook as I tried to put the key inside the lock.

"Are you cold?" Kevin asked as the key rattled against the brass door handle.

"No. Why?" I finally managed to fit the key in its hole and turned the lock.

"Because you're shaking like a leaf."

"Really? I hadn't noticed."

"For God's sake, Sarah, stop pretending that you're okay. You're obviously not coping."

"I'm handling it. I'm fine." I couldn't face the thought that Kevin may be right. Was I coping?

"Then why are you freaking out?"

"I'm not freaking out." I refused to admit that I was bloody scared. "I need a drink, what about you?"

"Ja, sure, why not."

I needed to forget the fear and the pain of my father's death. I'd always been a supporter of the 'fake it till you make it' club. If it meant faking being a sex kitten to get through the night, then that's what I would do. I left him standing at my front door and sauntered off into my kitchenette. I had an over-sized fridge I'd inherited from my sister. There wasn't space for a proper oven in the kitchen; instead I had a microwave and a hotplate on the only counter. Despite the cramped space, it was done tastefully. The cupboards were dark wood with silver handles and the counter tops had a black marble finish.

I opened the ancient fridge and took out a half-full bottle of wine that Kevin and I had opened a few nights previously. Before my life changed, forever. I felt him come up behind me. His hand snaked its way up and under my tight black camisole. His lips caressed my neck and found their way to my ear lobes. He nibbled the lobes gently. I gasped. His hand gripped my breast: fingernails bit into my flesh. He was breathing hard. I slammed the fridge door closed and turned into his embrace. My lips found his as he pushed me back, hard against the fridge. I managed to keep a tight hold of the bottle. Pushing him away, I took a swig of wine and handed it to him. While he drank, I pulled the camisole over my head. His eyes watched me as he took another drink. I played with my nipples and then slid my left hand down, slowly, towards my crotch. He liked to watch. He put the wine bottle on the counter and then kissed me hard. I pushed him against the wall and pulled away from him. Undoing the top button of my jeans, my fingers found their way down. I pulled my hand back out and let him lick the juices from my fingertips.

I turned and walked towards the bedroom. I heard his shoes tapping on the tiles as he followed me. I knew Kevin would drive the fear and pain I felt, deep in my bones, out of my body. I surrendered every inch of me.

*

Kevin watched as Sarah's chest rose and fell with her every breath. He had places to go and another girl to do. He checked his watch and swore under his breath when he realised that he would be late. Switching his phone back on, he checked for messages. She hadn't called. Sarah was the one who called. Denise never did. Sarah needed and wanted him – especially now – but it was Denise who drove him wild. She didn't care if he called her or not. It made her even sexier. He was never sure of her, but he knew exactly where he stood with Sarah, which made it all too easy.

He climbed out of bed, trying not to wake her and put on

his clothes. He hated sneaking out, but he wanted to avoid seeing the hurt look on Sarah's face. He also didn't feel like answering any questions.

The remote Sarah gave him came in handy as he drove out the gate. Denise didn't live far, which was lucky for him. Hopefully he wasn't too late. He sped down the road driving straight over some of the traffic circles.

Denise's complex was on a corner in Rugby Street. It only took him five minutes to get there. There were advantages to seeing two girls who lived so close to each other. There were also disadvantages, but the pros outweighed the cons. Luckily Denise didn't seem to have any problems with his relationship with Sarah, though he knew that Sarah wouldn't feel the same way. She had told him once, when he'd suggested a threesome, that she didn't share her toys. That had put an end to his idea of having both Sarah and Denise in the same bed together. It would have been extremely cool. But maybe it could still happen if he played his cards right.

He pushed the button on the complex intercom for Denise's place and waited. It was a few minutes past two in the morning. A man's voice answered which was a surprise. He hadn't been expecting that. There was a bit of a commotion. It sounded like two people kissing and then he heard Denise telling someone to go back to bed and wait.

"Hello," Denise sounded husky.

"Hey, you. I'm sorry I'm late."

"Late?" she sounded confused. "Did we have plans?"

"Ja." It was now Kevin's turn to sound confused. "I said I'd come by after I'd ditched Sarah."

"Oh." There was a pause, some more commotion and then Denise giggled. "Well, I made other plans."

"Oh."

"Goodnight."

The intercom went off. Kevin stood outside the gate, and listened to the sound of his car engine, wanting Denise more than he'd ever wanted her before.

*

Denise smiled. It was a beautiful smile. Carol's heart

stopped when she looked like that. She watched as Denise put the handset for the intercom back in its cradle.

"And?" Carol asked.

"Things are looking good," Denise said as she stroked Carol's face.

"Ladies," some guy Denise had picked up a few days earlier, called from the bedroom.

"How much longer are we keeping this idiot?" Carol asked.

"Would you keep your voice down?" Denise said.

"I'm waiting," the idiot shouted.

"In a minute," Carol shouted back.

"He goes tonight." Denise kissed her slowly. "I promise."

"Good."

"Kevin's ready for us," Denise said between kisses. "But are you ready?"

"I think so." Carol's voice sounded unsure in her own ears.

"That's not good enough."

"I will be," Carol sighed. "I promise."

*

Carol sat on the old leather couch. Her new psychiatrist stank of Old Spice. She hated the smell. The thought of ripping his throat out appealed to her. It made her smile.

"Tell me about Dr. Phillips," the new doctor said.

"What's to tell?" she said. "He couldn't keep his dick in his pants."

"And now he's losing his license to practice," he said.

"I guess he won't be screwing another patient then, will he," she smirked.

"And how does that make you feel?"

She hated it when they asked that question. They didn't care how she felt. The only reason they asked was because they didn't know what else to say.

His pen scratched on the notepad. The sound irritated her.

"Are you recording our session?" she asked.

"Is that a problem for you?"

"No," she sighed. "Don't worry about it. I just wondered why you needed to scribble notes if you're recording it all."

"Would you rather I didn't take any notes?"

"I don't care what you do."

"What would you like to talk about today?"

"Are you gay?"

"Excuse me?"

"Are you a homosexual?"

"Yes, I am." He blushed. She smiled.

"Does that bother you?" he asked.

"No," she said. "It explains why Dr. Phillips referred me to you."

"And why do you think that is?"

"Since you prefer dicks to chicks, I can't seduce you."

"Did you seduce him?"

She stood up and walked towards the window.

"No." She stared out with unseeing eyes.

"Why are you here, Carol?"

"Because of Dr. Phillips."

"Why were you seeing Dr. Phillips?"

"You have my file." She looked over her shoulder at him. "Doesn't that tell you?"

"There's not a lot in here."

"My mother felt I needed therapy."

"Why?"

"She caught me with the next-door neighbour's daughter."

"How old were you?"

"Sixteen." She carried on staring out of the window.

A soft buzzing sound came from the small clock on his desk.

"Our time is up," he said as he stood up. She was at least a head taller than him. She liked being able to look down at him.

"I'll see you same time next week," he said.

"I'll try not to kill anybody before then." She enjoyed the look of confusion cross his face. She grinned. She was going to enjoy her sessions with Dr. Brink.

2

Some bloody wanker was mowing the lawn. I poked my head out from under the duvet. It wasn't even half-past seven in the morning. I rolled over. Kevin was gone. He'd probably let himself out sometime during the night. Typical. He was hardly ever there when I woke up. I wasn't sure how I felt about his not being there in the morning. There were times when I was relieved and then there were times when I was insulted. Sometimes it simply hurt.

Sundays were the only day of the week I could sleep in and as luck would have it, I was woken up early on most Sundays. It sucked. I stretched and enjoyed a good yawn. There's nothing better in the morning than a good spread-eagle stretch and a wide, open-mouthed yawn, followed by a cup of strong coffee. Unfortunately, due to an irritating ulcer, I couldn't enjoy a good cup of hot coffee. I had to settle for a mug of green tea instead. I missed the serious caffeine boost.

I rolled out of bed and waddled into the kitchen. The tiled floor was cold against my bare feet. Memories from the night before made me shiver. The freak's face kept flashing in front of my eyes as I waited for the kettle to boil. I shook my head and told myself I was being stupid.

I hoped that I'd imagined it all, but I wasn't ready to admit that I was completely round the bend either. If I hadn't imagined it all then what was going on? Was I as nutty as a fruitcake?

The kettle clicked and interrupted my thoughts.

The tinkling of a bell announced Gypsy's presence.

Gypsy was what my vet called a miracle cat. When she found her way into my life, I was living in Pretoria. I'd been on my way to the dvd place on the next block when I heard a cat mewing. It was so soft I almost missed it. The sound came from under a bush. Some sick bastard had stubbed out cigarettes on her. Most of her fur had been burnt off and her stomach cut open. She'd been dumped in the park across from the building where I lived. The park was notorious for satanic rituals. She just lay there, fighting for her life. I forgot all about returning the dvd and sprinted back to my flat, fetched a towel and my car keys. I hoped she would still be alive when I got back.

She was still under the bush, looking at me with beautiful, pain-filled eyes.

The park gave me the creeps even in broad daylight. It was directly across the road from an old Catholic church. Nobody walked around there at night and they walked quickly through it during the day. People never sat on the benches on a Sunday after church and children never played on the swings.

I wrapped her in the towel. She didn't hiss or claw me. Maybe she'd lost too much blood to put up a fight.

The vet, Dr Venter, was a few blocks away from my mother's and he'd been the family vet since I was a little girl. His house was attached to his practice. He was always available for late night emergencies and over weekends.

Taking one look at Gypsy, he took her straight into his operating theatre. His assistant told me to go home. They'd call me.

He fixed her up and I took her home a couple of days later. She's been with me ever since. Sometimes I wonder who looks after whom. She kept me sane at some of the worst moments of my life.

I took a sip of green tea and again missed being able to have a cup of coffee.

My phone rang. Thanks to caller ID, I knew it was Kevin. Weird, he never called that early. I answered. There was no 'Hello' from him, but then there hardly ever was. That was one of the things that attracted me to him. He just didn't care what people thought.

"I can't make it tonight. We're having a family thing."

"That's cool. I've got stuff to do anyway."

"Cool." The phone went dead before I could say anything else.

The family thing meant he was invited to have dinner with his parents and I was officially not invited. His family didn't like me very much and made no bones about it. Personally, I didn't think very much of them, either. They took dysfunctional to a whole new level.

I decided that an early night might be just what the doctor ordered. I was safe at home. No weirdos, drunks or figments of my imagination trying to scare me, would be able to hurt me in my own home. At least I hoped not.

*

Sunday nights were relaxing. Kevin and I usually had plans, which ended up being cancelled thanks to his family, so I spent them alone. Which was, actually, pretty good. I was better at being alone than being with other people. Kevin on the other hand needed people. In the months that we'd been together I'd probably spent more time with other people than I had in my entire life. Kevin couldn't understand my need for time on my own and I never got his constant need to have people around him. He was the life of the party and I wasn't. Because of that I knew our relationship couldn't last, though there were times that I hoped it would.

It was not the night to worry about another doomed relationship. I decided that I was going to enjoy every minute of my much-needed alone time. A glass or two of red wine and a good film was exactly what I needed. The eight o'clock movie on M-Net was Secret Window. Another good thriller: not that my life wasn't thrilling enough.

Johnny Depp was his usual sexy self, but it was a bit strange seeing him in the role of a delusional killer. Supper was a simple green salad. I couldn't quite stomach anything more. I'd lost my appetite since the night my mother called to tell me that my father had killed himself.

The movie ended with Johnny saying something about endings, and that his particular ending was a very good one. Maybe Kevin and I would have a good ending to our story.

I took my half-empty glass of wine to bed with me. I had every intention of reading a few pages of Micki Pistorius's "Fatal Females", but was only half way down the page before my eyes closed.

I rolled over and managed to switch off the bedside lamp

before falling asleep. Gypsy snuggled up in her usual spot. I always slept on my stomach which left the backs of my legs free for her to perch herself on. She usually slept with her head on my arse. I drifted off into a deep sleep and dreams floated in and out.

Gypsy hissed. My heart pounded. There was something in the room with us. Gypsy bolted off the bed. I could still hear her hissing and screeching from under the bed. I rolled onto my back and looked around to see what it was. I thought it was another cat from next door. But a voice at the back of my mind screamed – RUN.

Shadows moved and took shape. I closed my eyes and blinked to clear my vision. There was something there: something with shape and form. It was coming for me. I wanted to scream but no sound came out. A hand came out of the shadows. It was a claw, not a hand. It grabbed my ankle. I felt its talon dig into my flesh.

"There's nothing there," I whispered. "It's just my imagination."

Another claw grabbed my other ankle. Using my legs, it pulled its way out of the darkness, coming closer towards me. Its head emerged out of the shadows. It looked at me, smiling. It was the man from the parking lot.

He slowly clawed his way up my body. A scream locked in my throat. I was paralysed with fear. The air in the room froze and time stood still.

His face was above mine and his breath stank of rotting flesh.

"Real enough for you?" He said with a grin. "I'm really going to enjoy our time together."

The weight of his body pressed down on me. I couldn't breathe. Cold, hard lips pressed down on mine. I closed my eyes. His sharp teeth bit into my lower lip and I tasted blood. His tongue slithered into my mouth. I bit down hard. And bit my own tongue. I opened my eyes. He was gone.

I switched on the bedside lamp and scanned the room. My heart was pumping ninety to the dozen. A cold sweat covered my body. My teeth chattered and I could still taste blood. My tongue and lip hurt like hell.

Gypsy jumped back onto the bed and made herself comfortable on my stomach. I tickled her under her chin with shaky fingers and she started to purr.

*

Kevin's parents were in high spirits. He hadn't seen them this happy in a long time. Denise sat between him and his sister Carol. He wasn't exactly sure how he felt about his sister and Denise holding hands under the table. He also had an inkling why Denise hadn't had any problem with his desire for a threesome. The fact that she seemed to like chicks was a definite turn on but, Denise doing Carol was a whole other story. He also doubted that his parents guessed at the relationship between their little girl and the woman they hoped he was seeing. He couldn't help but wonder if that titbit of information would change their mind about Sarah. Although, he somehow doubted it would.

Sarah had made the unforgivable mistake of arguing religion with his devout Catholic parents. He had told her not to, but Sarah couldn't help herself. She'd decided that his parents were narrow-minded and antiquated in their beliefs; his parents had branded her a heretic who should be burnt at the stake. They settled for banning her from all family dinners.

Sarah's big mouth always landed her in trouble. It was one of the things that had attracted him to her in the first place. Now, it was one of the things he found the most irritating.

Denise smiled at him, her brown eyes twinkling. His gaze drifted down from her eyes to her low-cut top. Denise moved her chair back a little so that he could get a better view. Then he noticed something else, and deliberately dropped his fork. Bending down to retrieve it, he saw Denise's hand up his sister's skirt. Part of him was disgusted, but his cock reacted without permission and stood at attention. He bumped his head on the edge of the table in his hurry to get away from his confusion. He didn't want to see Denise pleasuring his sister. He wanted her hand down his pants, not up his sister's skirt.

Carol's smile was wide and her eyes glistened with pleasure. His parents were oblivious. It came as a shock when he felt a hand on his thigh. Fingers travelled lightly upwards towards the zip of his jeans. She must have read his mind. He glanced at Denise who was talking and smiling as though nothing was going on. Surely his parents would pick up that Denise didn't have any hands on the round table and wasn't eating anything, or that their daughter wasn't saying anything or that her breathing was a little funny. All thoughts vanished as he felt Denise's hand inside his jocks, freeing his cock.

He couldn't breathe. He felt dirty and his cock got harder. He wanted to burst. He had to get out of there. He jumped off his chair, causing his parents to stare at him. Thankfully he had the presence of mind to hold the napkin over his swollen appendage and unzipped jeans.

"I'm sorry. I forgot I had to do something very important," he stammered as he backed away from the table and knocked over his chair. "I have to go." He turned and walked away, holding his jeans up, fighting the urge to run and ignoring his chair on the floor.

"What's wrong with him?" he heard Carol ask as he opened the front door. He closed the door behind him. The cool night air was pleasant against his hot face.

"Can't take the heat?" Denise stood behind him, a smirk on her face.

"What game are you playing at?" he asked.

"I'm just having some fun. Don't you want to have some fun?" she asked looking up at him. Her eyes seemed to glow. Her fingers found his still-unzipped pants and started caressing him.

"It's sick. Fingering my sister and ..." he couldn't finish his sentence. She was nibbling his ear and her hand was inside his jocks, rubbing him slowly. He couldn't help himself. He wanted her so much that he felt his head was about to explode. His lips found hers and he gave in.

*

Carol listened to Kevin's heavy breathing from behind the door, which Denise had left open for her. She heard him groan and couldn't help smiling.

"Is everything alright?" her mother asked.

"Everything's perfect, Mom," Carol said with a wink and tried to cover her surprise at finding her mother standing next to her.

"I didn't mean them."

"I know you didn't."

"Tell me about this Dr. Brink."

"He's gay, so you don't have to worry about another scandal."

"Gay! I didn't realise he was one of those." She sighed. "Please don't say anything in front of your brother and father." A tear threatened to melt the icy grip her mother had around her emotions. "I've worked very hard to make sure that they never know about that sordid affair of yours."

"Don't worry; they'll never hear it from me."

"As long as it suits you, they won't." She shook her head. "I know you well enough. The moment you think it will cause them pain, you won't hesitate to tell them."

"That's great, Mom," she said, keeping her voice even. "It's so good to know that my mother thinks so highly of me."

"What did you expect after everything you've done to this family?" her mother retorted over her shoulder, as she walked away.

"Some unconditional love would have been a nice change," she whispered.

The sounds of kissing drifted towards her from outside and her parents fake-happy conversational voices enveloped her in hot, angry, isolation. She couldn't breathe.

"Are you okay?" Denise asked. Carol hadn't heard her come back inside.

"I'll be fine."

"You will be." She nodded. "I promise."

"Where's Kevin?"

"I sent him home." Denise smiled. "I've got him right where we want him."

"Good."

Her pain and anger melted away with the knowledge that it would all be over soon. She just had to be patient.

3

The sun woke up as I made my way to work along William Nicol and turned onto Sandton Drive. The Sandton skyline loomed in the dark ahead of me and the morning DJ was making a noise on 5FM. Finally he shut up and started playing some music. Madonna's latest hit thumped through the back speakers.

I pulled into the office garage. I was usually the first person there, so it was deserted, except for the half-asleep security guards. I drove down to the basement and parked in my designated spot.

The nightmare was still fresh in my mind. I hadn't been able to get much sleep after that. I needed to talk to someone, someone who was probably just as whacky as me; someone who would understand. There were a few options to choose from. Most of my friends were on the strange side.

The sound of my old Golf's door slamming reverberated around the empty basement.

"What is it with me and deserted parking lots this week?" I asked myself aloud. "Great, now I'm talking to myself."

The overhead lights flickered on and off. It was like being in an empty nightclub. I tried to ignore the mounting fear tingling up my spine. I made my way to the glass doors that separated the lifts from the basement parking area and swiped my card across the electronic reader. It buzzed and the lock on the glass door opened. I stepped into the lobby and the door slammed back into place, locking behind me. I felt a lot safer.

I pressed the button and waited for the lift, which was notoriously slow, to make it's way down to me. It finally arrived and the doors opened at an annoying snail's pace. I stepped inside and pressed for the third floor. I checked my reflection in the mirror which had a jagged crack running across the right hand corner.

I ran my fingers through my hair and my reflection started to change. It wasn't my face any more. It became a distorted jumble of features swirling around. I started feeling dizzy.

Another image formed in the mirror. At first I couldn't make out what it was. My heart pounded in my chest. My hands shook. I closed my eyes and took a deep breath. The face in the mirror was his.

The man from my nightmares leered at me. I sank to my knees and smothered the urge to let out a blood-curdling scream. The last thing I needed was for a security guard to show up. It would be all over the building that there was a crazy woman working on the third floor.

The sound of his laughter bounced off the walls.

"That's right," he said. "Fall to your knees like a good little girl. And while you're down there ..."

The lift stopped and the doors opened. I was on my feet and almost fell in my haste to get out. The doors closed behind me. My body shook and my heart pounded harder.

"It wasn't real," I whispered to myself. "It was just another hallucination."

I took a few deep breaths and prepared myself for taking a step forward.

My hands were still shaking as I turned the key in the lock and punched in the code to disable the alarm.

The office was in darkness. Lights shone in through the windows from the streets below and the offices across the road. I used to love having the office to myself in the early hours of the morning. The view of the JSE when it was all lit up was stunning. I could see lights coming on at Nedcor: workaholics making their first cups of coffee. It wasn't fair. I also wanted a cup.

I switched on the lights. They flickered above my head and flashed on down the passage, and into the offices. I locked the main door behind me and made my way to my open-plan office. The call centre, which I ran, would be full and noisy in an hour's time.

I started my day by testing all the equipment. People would be calling in and asking questions soon.

One of the small spotlights in the ceiling had a habit of flickering on and off. It normally didn't bother me, but today, it started to make me a little uneasy. All the sounds I heard every morning had me wondering if there was something else in the room with me. I couldn't wait for the rest of the staff to start trickling in. I still felt as though I was being watched.

Jessie, the accountant, usually arrived shortly after I did, just before seven. I just had to stay sane for another half hour.

She was someone I could talk to. I only confided in her if I wanted an honest, no-holds-barred opinion. Jessie didn't believe in pulling her punches. She always told it how she saw it, which was usually spot on.

I dreaded discussing my hallucinations with her, but I needed her honesty. I needed her brand of caring.

I stared at the fountain down below. My hazy reflection stared back at me from a dirty window. I felt something come up behind me. A second reflection appeared in the window. My heart pounded again: at that rate I was going to die of a heart attack before I hit thirty.

I felt something on my shoulder and almost jumped out of my skin.

"Are you okay?" I heard Jessie's voice ask through the noise of blood rushing through my eardrums.

"I think you just took ten years off my expected lifespan," I managed to mumble, as I tried to calm down my heart and doubled over, while I tried to catch my breath.

"A little jumpy this morning," she said with a cocked eyebrow and a slight grin. "How was the funeral?" she asked as she pushed me out of the way and opened the window. The sky was tinted in light pinks and oranges as, the sun climbed over the top of the Hilton on Rivonia Road. Jessie dug in her over-sized handbag and pulled out a pack of cigarettes.

All I managed was a lop-sided smile in reply.

"I think you might need one of these more than I do," she said as she tapped one out of the soft pack.

"You know what?" I said. "You may be right."

"Right, like you would actually have a smoke?"

"Today I think I need one."

"Okay, for you to want to smoke, something serious is obviously going on. You didn't even want a smoke when you got the news about your Dad."

"Yep." I choked up. I tried hard to swallow my tears.

"Do you want to talk about it?" Her smile was kind. The floodgates burst and the tears that had built up over the weekend overflowed.

"I think I'm losing my mind," I spluttered out between sobs.

"What's going on? Did something happen at the funeral?"

"I wish it was that simple." I said and gave her an abbreviated version of the events that took place over the weekend. She just stared out of the window smoking her cigarette without saying a word for what seemed like an eternity. Tears rolled down my face. I didn't bother to wipe them away. I thought about taking her up on the offer for a smoke, but decided that coughing my lungs out would only add to my misery. She finished her smoke and flicked the butt out of the window.

"Sweetie, I don't know what to say," she said, still staring out of the window. "This is way out of my realm of experience."

"I know. It's just that I needed to talk to someone about it."

"If you'd been on drugs while you saw all this stuff …" She tapped another cigarette out of the pack. "I'd say don't take that shit again. But this …"

"You know I don't touch that stuff. I definitely don't need drugs to have hallucinations." I tried to smile. "As proven this weekend."

"There's a lot of stuff that you haven't allowed yourself to deal with. Your father only died a few days ago and you didn't get to reconcile before he died." She lit the cigarette and took a couple of puffs. "Maybe this is your subconscious asking for help."

"Well, my subconscious has a messed up way of asking for help."

"I can't believe I'm about to say this," she said as she turned and looked at me.

"Say what?"

"Your sister may be right for once."

"Right about what, exactly?" I took a deep breath.

"Look, I know your sister has been pushing you to see a shrink for grief counselling and family issues, but I think having hallucinations may warrant a session on the couch."

"I can't afford it."

"That's a lousy excuse." She blew smoke out of the window. "Your mental health is the most important thing right now and you need to find the money to take care of yourself."

I didn't have an answer for that. She was right, but I didn't want to expose myself to a total stranger like that. The thought of telling someone else what was happening sent shivers through me.

"I don't need to see a shrink." I wasn't ready to admit that I was losing it. "I've got you and our early morning sessions."

She looked at me without saying anything. I couldn't hold her gaze. She took one last drag from her cigarette, blew out of the window again and eyed me with hard, penetrating intensity. The scrutiny made me uncomfortable.

"You need professional help." She stubbed out her cigarette on the windowsill and flicked it out into the morning breeze.

*

Kevin's laughter reverberated through the room. His sister, Carol, sat on the arm of his chair and played with his dark hair. They could have been twins. They both had dark-brown, bordering on black, hair and wide-set brown eyes. Kevin was what most women would classify as sexy, but what made Kevin attractive had the opposite effect for Carol. Being tall and athletic only served to make her appearance masculine.

The party was in full swing and I wasn't sure why I'd been invited. Kevin's group of friends were an incestuous bunch who hung out with each other and only dated within the group. Kevin had broken a few of their strict rules when he started seeing me. They tolerated my presence at their parties but, whenever we went out, they let me know that I was still the outsider. It would take a long time for them to accept me.

I watched them from the other side of the room. Kevin's elbow rested lightly on Carol's thigh. She laughed at one of his jokes. I watched in silence, sipping on my large glass of red wine. Another woman I hadn't seen before, made her way across the room towards them and sat on the other arm of his chair. As I watched I realised that she was a friend of Carol's. From the way they laughed and chatted together, I gathered that Kevin also knew her well. I didn't like that idea.

That nagging voice at the back of my mind started to make itself heard over the usual white noise that was commonplace in my head. My stomach started to react to the scene playing out in front of me. There was something about the way this woman looked at Kevin; in the way she touched him. It was intimate. The voice started screaming that there was something going on.

I was jealous and I hated being jealous. As if dealing with my father's suicide and going crazy wasn't enough to deal with, I had to add an unfaithful boyfriend to the mix as well. When I screwed up the courage and found a shrink, I would have a lot to talk about.

I walked over to the intimate huddle. I was going to put a stop to it.

"Hey, babe," Kevin greeted me.

"Mind if I join in?" I tried to sound nonchalant. "Or is this for members only?"

"Members only," the other woman replied. Her brown eyes sparkled.

"I'm sorry. Have we met?" I asked.

"No, we haven't and, hopefully, we never will again."

Carol giggled like a schoolgirl.

"Excuse me?" I couldn't believe the audacity.

"Now, now, ladies. Play nice." Kevin stood up and led me across the room. "What's your problem?" he asked once we were alone in the hallway.

"What's my problem?"

"Ja. Your problem?"

"I'm sorry, I didn't realise I wasn't allowed to talk to my boyfriend at a party."

"You need to chill."

"What?"

"Look, Denise is an old friend and your jealousy is not something I'm going to tolerate." He crossed his arms over his chest. "So I think you should go home and I'll call you in the morning."

"Don't bother," I said and walked away. Tears stung my eyes. Humiliation settled in my stomach. Why did it always have to hurt so much? And what was it about that woman that made Kevin act like such a shit? I asked myself as I sat in my car. The music from the party drifted out towards me.

The music changed. There was a whisper mingled in with the beat of the drums. I strained to hear it. Did I hear my name? I listened harder. It sounded like one of those ridiculous cheers from high school. The whisper got louder and I could make out what was being said. My breath caught in my throat. My misery about Kevin and the party was replaced by shock and indignation. I couldn't believe what I was hearing.

"Kevin, Kevin, he's our man.
He'll put Sarah's head in a can.
Sarah, Sarah, she's our chick.
She'll slice off Kevin's dick."

The whisper became a chant and got louder and louder. It wasn't coming from the party anymore. It was coming from somewhere inside my car. The radio was off. I turned around in my seat to have a look at the back. His face came at me and his stinking breath hit my nose as he shouted "BOO!"

Then all was quiet again. Only the soft melodic music from the party drifted on the evening breeze.

*

Kevin stared at the doorway where Sarah had just stormed out. His hands shook. Denise's hands walked up his back, between his shoulder blades.

"Did you have to be such a bitch?" he asked, not looking at her.

27

"Oh, come on," she breathed into his ear. "She's weak, needy and pathetic. It's not my fault she can't stand up for herself."

"So what if she's needy." Kevin turned to look at her. "At least she gives a shit."

"And I don't?"

"I don't think you do."

"I think you need to ask yourself if you actually care about little Miss Pathetic, who is probably still sitting outside in her car right now, crying her little blue eyes out." Her hand found its way to his crotch and she grabbed him. "Or do you want to have fun with me."

All he could feel was her hand on his cock. He didn't want to deal with Sarah's emotional tantrums. Playing with Denise was a lot easier.

*

Sarah's exit didn't create much of a stir; her exits never did. What did excite interest though, was Denise and Kevin.

"What's going on between Denise and Kevin?" Rosemary, the group gossip, asked.

"What do you think?" Carol replied, as she stared at the bedroom door that Denise had closed behind her, shutting Carol out. She and Kevin had snuck in there a few moments earlier. It was something that everybody had noticed. It was something that Denise made sure everybody noticed.

"Does this mean he's finally getting rid of that little Miss Know-it-all?"

"I don't know what my brother plans to do about Sarah."

"I think it's high time he dumped that cow."

"You think everybody who's smarter than you should be dumped."

"She's not smarter than me."

"You just keep telling yourself that," Carol said and ignored the indignant look on Rosemary's face and the sound of her high heels retreating, as she skulked back towards the party.

"What's taking so long?" Carol mumbled. "She should have been done by now."

The sound of Denise's laughter slithered through the wooden door. Her heart sank. A million different 'what if?' questions ran amuck, causing damage.

"This has to work," she whispered. "It just has to."

The door opened. Carol jumped back to avoid having her toes crushed.

"What are you doing here?" Kevin asked. His face was red and his shirt wasn't buttoned up properly.

"I ...um ..." she stumbled over her own tongue.

"She's been standing guard," Denise said. "Making sure nobody disturbed us. Weren't you sweetie?"

"Yes. That's exactly what I was doing," she smiled.

She looked over Kevin's shoulder hoping to see something in Denise's face that would stop the storm raging within her.

Denise nodded and smiled. That was all she needed. All thoughts of failure vanished. Everything was on track. Everything was as it should be.

4

Kevin called the next day and we both pretended that nothing had happened. We pretended that everything was fine.

"We're having a family dinner tonight," Kevin said.

"Another one?" I said, trying not to sound irritated.

"Ja," he sighed. "Mom and Carol are having issues. When they have issues, Mom insists on family dinners."

"I see," I lied. I didn't understand.

"You're invited," he said.

"What did you say?" I couldn't have heard him right.

"You're invited."

"I thought I was permanently banned."

"I thought so too," he sighed again. "My mother's giving you a second chance. Please don't screw this up."

"Gee, thanks for the vote of confidence." I spat the words out and tried to quiet the tears that threatened to shatter the fragile composure I was fighting to keep.

"Look, I'm sorry. I didn't mean it that way. I'll see you tonight at my folk's place," he said. "Do you remember how to get there?"

"How could I forget," I said. "See you later." The phone clicked before I could get the last word out.

My hands shook. I hadn't seen his parents since they threw me out during one of their family dinners.

I couldn't help but wonder why his mother wanted me there. The calculating bitch never did anything without an ulterior motive. What could she possibly hope to gain by my attending a family dinner? It didn't make any sense. Nothing to do with his family made sense. I prayed that nothing happened during the dinner.

*

I arrived five minutes late. I hated being late. I had a feeling that it would be used against me. The front door was open except for the security gate which blocked my entrance. I could hear laughter. Somebody must have said something very funny.

"Hello," I shouted through the bars. No-one answered. They kept on laughing.

"Hello," I shouted a little louder and then waited for the laughter to quieten down.

"Hello," I shouted once again.

"There's no need to scream," Kevin's mother said as she walked down the passage towards me.

"I'm sorry," I said. "I didn't mean to. I didn't think you could hear me."

"Oh, we heard you the first time," Evelyn said.

Bitch. I wanted to scream. Instead I bit my tongue.

"Hey babe," Kevin smiled as he came up behind his mother. "You're late."

"That's because I've been standing out here."

"Oh. Mom said it was open."

"It wasn't." I tried to smile. I tried to soften the irritation in my voice, but couldn't. I didn't want to be there and I wouldn't be able to hide it.

Evelyn gave a half-hearted smile as she unlocked the gate.

"My mistake," she said as she pulled the key out of the lock and pushed it open. "But if you'd been on time it would have been unlocked." The smile never left her face.

I took a step back and managed to avoid being hit as it swung out towards me.

I stepped past his mother and walked into an uncomfortable silence.

Denise stood in the middle of the room. I thought about running away but instead, took a deep breath, squared my shoulders and walked towards her.

"Hello," I said, thrusting my hand out in an inane gesture. "I'm Sarah. I think we met last night."

"Yes," she said, ignoring my hand and staring over my shoulder at Kevin.

My hand retreated. I should have stayed at home.

I caught a glimpse of myself in the mirror his parents had hanging in the dining room. Something about my reflection bothered me. I took a closer look. Blood pooled in my eyes, ran out of the corners, and down my cheeks. I closed my eyes and shook my head. When I opened them again my reflection was back to normal. No one noticed the panicked look on my face or that I'd turned a few shades paler. I looked back at the mirror and was greeted by my nightmare vision grinning at me. I looked away and tried to focus on Kevin who was being pawed by Denise and his sister. There was something very strange about that relationship. I stole another glance at the mirror, but he was gone. My heart rate slowed down a bit, but I couldn't get rid of the queasy feeling in my stomach. I wasn't sure if that was because I was losing my mind or because I was nervous about dinner.

The round dining room table was opulently set. Evelyn had gone all out. She must have dug out her best silver for the occasion. She'd even put out those little silver place settings with name tags on them. Denise sat next to Kevin and I was placed next to Carol. Kevin's mother sat on the other side of him, placing herself between us. His father sat between Carol and Denise. Subtlety was not one of Evelyn's strong points. Now I understood why I'd been invited.

I was not there to redeem myself or be given a second chance, as Kevin had put it. I was there to be put in my place.

I spent the evening slowly dying inside as I watched Denise and Kevin laughing at each other's jokes. I watched Kevin's family interact with and accept Denise whilst I was ignored.

Every time I tried to assert myself in the conversation, Denise or Carol would talk over me and what I wanted to say would be lost. Eventually I gave up and simply listened with a stupid smile on my face.

Evelyn may have won the battle but she hadn't won the war. It would take a lot more to get rid of me.

*

Kevin called the next morning.

"You were really quiet at dinner last night," he said

"Didn't have much to say." I didn't know what else to tell him. He wouldn't believe, or understand, if I tried to explain things to him. He would simply have said that I was imagining things once again. It was easier to just let it go.

"Okay, but that's not like you."

"I know. I was just having a quiet moment. I was listening for a change. That's what you wanted me to do, wasn't it?"

"Ja. I guess," he said. "I wasn't expecting you to just shut up."

"You asked me to behave myself."

"True." He took a deep breath. "We're having another one tonight. Carol and Mom are still having issues so I won't be able to see you this evening."

"That's okay," I said. "Have a good one." I wanted to cry as I put the phone down. I took a deep breath and then exhaled slowly. I had to be strong. I wasn't the clingy type or at least I didn't want to be. I could handle another night on my own.

I decided I wasn't losing my mind. I refused to surrender my sanity. It was obviously my strange way of dealing with my father's suicide. That was all there was to it. I was putting the incidents behind me. I didn't need to spend a fortune on a shrink, and I could deal with everything on my own. I'd always been good at handling my problems on my own.

I could carry on with my life as though nothing had happened. That's what I told myself. I would simply ignore any further episodes the same way I had the night before.

Most of my girlfriends lived in Pretoria and it was a pain, having to drive there and then spend the night at my Mom's, or on one of their couches. I decided that a girlie evening just for me was in order.

I could listen to Evanescence and sing along at the top of my voice to My Immortal without having to worry about Kevin, or anybody else for that matter, laughing at me.

I could dance around the room and munch popcorn while watching some chick-flick like Tomb Raider, Electra or Mr & Mrs Smith. I had it all planned out. The best-laid plans and all that stuff. I didn't see it coming.

Later that evening Gypsy was curled up on the couch, watching me, while I twirled around the room, dancing like a mad woman. I danced through most of the CD and collapsed breathless on the couch, almost knocking Gypsy off her perch. She was not impressed. In her disgust she stretched, jumped off the couch and made a dash for the bathroom.

She hissed and suddenly changed direction, darting out of the bathroom and into the bedroom.

"Crazy cat," I said and made my way around my coffee table, to the TV cabinet, and decided to watch Jennifer Garner in Electra. I'd somehow got it into my head that I wanted a body like that and that I could get it from watching Alias reruns and my Electra DVD. Get a great body through osmosis. I should patent the idea. Both the 'Alias' woman and Electra were strong. I admired their strength. Perhaps it was that strength instead of the great body that I hoped to gain from them. I needed it now more than ever.

Gypsy pulled a disappearing act. Normally she would snuggle up against me while I lay on the couch, but she was nowhere in sight.

I watched it from beginning to end, only pausing to put a packet of buttered popcorn in the microwave and pour myself a glass of red wine. That was my supper for the night. I was simply too lazy to cook anything else. I guess some two-minute noodles would have been just as easy, but popcorn seemed like a better idea.

The movie ended with Electra walking away from her childhood home, victorious: another good ending. I turned off the TV and popped the DVD into its box. It was almost eleven o'clock. Time for bed. I switched on the bathroom light and screamed.

There was so much blood. I'd never seen so much blood. The floor slammed into my knees. I tried not to throw up as the horror hit me in the stomach. Gypsy was splayed open, like a chicken, on top of the shower door. Her face dangled between her two front paws like a lifeless doll. I could see her back paws dangling on the other side of the glass. Blood ran down on either side.

Rocking back and forth, tears ran down my face. This couldn't be. I couldn't believe that the little creature that had been my loyal companion all these years had been butchered.

But by whom? I was the only one there. Different scenarios ran around my chaotic mind, each one more absurd than the other. It took me some time to realise that there was something written on the mirror in what I could only assume was Gypsy's blood. All it said was SOON.

Soft fur rubbed against my arm. I looked down and Gypsy looked back up at me. I looked back into the bathroom with incomprehension. No blood. No dead Gypsy. White tiles gleamed in the bright light. There was nothing on the mirror. I closed my eyes and shook my head. I opened my eyes and the room was as it should have been. No blood in sight. Gypsy climbed onto my lap and pounded into my flesh with her claws, making herself comfortable on my bare legs. I didn't feel it as her claws scratched me. I carried on kneeling on the cold tiles, stroking her and staring at the white tiles.

*

The lawn mower man was at it again. He didn't even give it a break on a public holiday. My head hurt. There was a weight on the back of my thighs. I looked around. Gypsy was curled up with her head resting on my bum. Thank God. It had all been a very bad nightmare. A nasty reaction to the wine? I must have had way too much too drink. The problem was, I only remembered having one glass. Granted it was on an empty stomach.

And speaking of stomachs, mine was telling me I had a serious hangover.

Gypsy stretched, yawned and then curled up again. Her paw stretched out. The thought of what happened, in what I hoped had been a dream, brought tears to my eyes. I tried to choke them back, unsuccessfully. I rolled over. Gypsy slid off my legs onto the emerald green duvet. She was not impressed with the disturbance. I had a claw mark on my left butt cheek to prove it. I gathered her up in my arms and pulled her tight against my chest. She allowed me to hug her for a few seconds before the claws came out and she scratched me.

"Watch the claws, cat," I said, as she scampered off and I checked out the damage to my skin. Bloody welts appeared on my pale wrists. I could do with some time in the sun. I was starting to look anaemic.

I kicked off the duvet, stretched, yawned and then padded with bare feet on cold tiles to the kitchen. I opened the fridge and surveyed the contents. The bottle of wine was still relatively full. That was weird. There wasn't anything else in the fridge that took my attention. I grabbed the milk and slammed the door closed.

Coffee. I needed a cup of strong coffee. I put on my Russell & Hobbs stainless steel kettle and put two heaped teaspoons of Ricoffy into my floral mug, followed by three spoons of sugar. Strong and sweet. That's what I needed. The red button on the kettle popped up and I poured the boiling water into the mug with shaky hands. The smell of coffee drifted up my nostrils. I felt better immediately. Nothing quite like an instant caffeine fix: especially since I wasn't allowed to drink it. There's nothing quite like forbidden fruit. I turned on the radio on my way out the front door. Thirty Seconds to Mars' The Kill thumped through the speakers.

The sun crept over the wall. My garden only enjoyed rays for a few hours each morning. The rest of the day it was all shadow. I loved sitting outside on the wire garden chair with my feet up on the table while I sipped my coffee. It was the best way to start off a day.

I propped my feet up on the table and enjoyed the feeling of the sun warming my bare legs. It drove the images of the night before out of my mind. I refused to go there. I tried not to, but the images were stubborn and wouldn't leave me alone.

No matter how hard I tried, I couldn't wipe the slate clean.

The 5FM DJ's were talking again. Why couldn't they just play music? I didn't want to listen to them talk. I wanted to listen to some good music. Forget myself in it. Mercifully they stopped talking and played some James Blunt. My father had loved his music. I choked back tears from the unexpected memory.

My phone started ringing in the bedroom. Gina had decided to interrupt my moment of self-torture. Gina was a self-proclaimed witch and psychic. She also believed she was a natural medium. I personally had yet to see any proof of these claims. Perhaps I'd get it now.

"You bored?" she asked in her deep, whisky voice.

"Not yet. But I probably will be in a couple of hours. Why?"

"I want to watch a movie."

"Cool, what time?"

"Half-past eleven at The Zone?"

"I'll be there."

And then she was gone. Our conversations on the phone were never long. Gina hated cell phones. She said they were poison.

The rest of the day would at least be a distraction, but the morning was a whole different ball game. I had to figure out what I was going to do with myself for the next few hours. I wasn't looking forward to being alone with my thoughts. Thoughts could be dangerous.

I realised that if things carried on like this I would have to call somebody. All thoughts of staying tough and facing things on my own flew out the window.

I then remembered Michael. Michael was an old friend and he had recently qualified as a psychiatrist. His practice was in Sandton. I hadn't spoken to him in months. I needed to talk to someone but didn't relish discussing my mental health with another friend.

*

Dark thunderclouds threatened overhead. This was one of the rainiest summers I'd experienced in the few years I'd been living in Joburg. The Zone in Rosebank was filled with shoppers and tourists. The African curio market was pumping with trade.

Gina was waiting for me at the bottom of the escalators leading up to the movies. She normally looked like a dominatrix, with a dash of gypsy fortune-teller mixed in. I called it the Gina look. But today she was dressed in jeans and a black v-neck T-shirt. I didn't even know that she owned a pair of jeans, let alone a T-shirt.

"What, no corset?" I asked, once the perfunctory hugs were done.

"Nope, they're all in the wash." She shrugged.

"At least you're wearing black."

"This is true." She looked down at her T-shirt, pulling it away from her curves. "It's the only colour in my wardrobe."

"Apparently black isn't a colour."

"Who cares?"

"I guess you don't."

"It doesn't even feature on my radar."

We decided to watch a horror movie: probably not the wisest choice. The lights were dim and the ads were playing at top volume as we found our seats. The hair on the back of my neck started to bristle. My skin crawled.

"It's damn cold in here," Gina whispered in my ear.

"That would explain the goose pimples harassing my skin," I whispered back. She smiled.

Shock smacked me at the back of my head. I spotted my other-worldly tormentor three rows down from us. He was standing in the aisle, staring at me with his bright-yellow eyes.

"There's a spirit attached to someone here."

"Really? Where?" My eyes never left him.

"I don't know. I'm just getting a bad vibe." She shivered.

"So you don't see that thing standing in the aisle over there." I gestured with my chin.

"Where?" Her voice was excited.

"Over there." I gestured with my chin again.

"You mean you're seeing things now?"

All I could do was nod my head.

"That is so cool."

I shook my head.

He climbed the stairs towards us. Reaching our row, he sat next to Gina and smiled at her. His sharp, pointed teeth resembled those of a wild animal. Fear crept into the muscles of my face.

"I like her," he said. "She's completely delusional. My kind of girl."

"Are you okay?" Gina asked. Her concern was evident from the look on her face.

Once again I could only manage to shake my head.

He helped himself to some of Gina's popcorn and then turned his head away from me and watched the screen.

"Snap out of it," I heard Gina whisper to me over the noise of the intro music for the movie. "There's nobody there who can hurt you."

I blinked my eyes but he was still there. Munching popcorn.

"It can't hurt you." Gina squeezed my hand.

It couldn't hurt me? Yeah, right.

I couldn't concentrate on the movie. The whole way through, all I could do was watch him eat Gina's popcorn. He laughed at parts where everybody else was screaming.

Afterwards Gina wanted to grab a bite to eat. She couldn't understand why her popcorn had disappeared so quickly. But I couldn't stomach the thought of food. I wanted to be alone, but couldn't help wondering if I would ever be alone again.

*

Denise and Carol lay naked on his bed kissing.

"I'm not screwing my sister," he whispered so that the other two wouldn't hear him. "She just happens to be screwing the same woman I am. That's all. I'm not bonking my sister."

"Stop whispering to yourself and get over here." Denise knelt on the bed. She was topless and her tits jiggled at him. Carol was staring at him with a weird smile stretched across her face. He hoped that this was as bizarre for her as it was for him.

Sarah had to be wrong about her. It pissed him off when Sarah made comments about his sister's feelings for him. She was his little sister. She wasn't in love with him. He didn't find her attractive. He was only doing it because Denise wanted him to. That was all. Carol was also there only because it was what Denise wanted. Sarah was wrong. She had to be.

The few steps he took towards the bed were the hardest he'd ever taken. His heart thumped in his throat. He wanted Denise. He hoped she was worth feeling disgusted with himself. As he took the last step he realised that he couldn't do it. He couldn't have sex, with his sister in the same bed. It went against every fibre of his being. If he went through with it there would be no turning back. He would never be able to look at Carol the same way again. It would turn their relationship into something ugly and dirty. He couldn't do it to either of them.

He turned away from them and grabbed his pants. It was bad enough that he'd seen her nude. It was an image he would never be able to wipe from his mind. Sex with her in the bed would be too much for him to handle.

"Baby, what's wrong?" Denise was standing behind him.

"I can't have sex with you and have my sister in the bed with us," Kevin said, as he turned to face her. She was the sexiest woman he'd ever seen.

"Baby, don't be like that," her voice was soft and pleading. "Carol and I have been lovers for a long time and this is one of my fantasies." She ran the tip of her index finger down his bare chest. "It's like a guy wanting to do it with twins. I just want to do it with a brother and sister. Why is that so wrong?"

"Because she's my sister. It's just freaky."

"Don't you want me?"

"Of course I want you. I think that's pretty obvious," he said looking down at his hard cock.

"Then do this for me and I promise I'll make it worth your while." She smiled up at him. It was the most amazing smile. It held the promise of incredible things, beyond his wildest imaginings.

She kissed him slowly and softly, enticing him back towards the bed. He didn't notice that his pants were back on the floor. She led him onto the bed. Denise kissed Carol and then blindfolded him.

He woke up to find both women curled up naked on either side of him. There was a feeling in his stomach that something terribly wrong had happened, and to make it worse he had enjoyed every moment of it. Flashes of Denise and his sister zoomed through his mind at an electrifying pace. He had crossed that line and there was no going back.

*

Carol sat on Dr. Brink's leather couch remembering. She had many memories circling around. Some she wanted to think about and others she wanted to ignore. Things she wanted to forget. Those were the memories that kept her awake at night. Those were the ones from which she woke up screaming and Denise would hold her till she fell asleep again.

"Tell me about your uncle?" Dr. Brink asked.

"I thought there wasn't much in my file."

"There isn't," he said. "Stop avoiding the issue, Carol. You're paying for these sessions, so you may as well get your money's worth."

"What does it say in my file about my uncle?"

"Just a note to probe deeper, about what happened with him."

"He's dead." She smiled. "He blew his brains out." Bigger smile.

"And that makes you happy?"

"Yes." Another smile.

"Why?"

There was a long pause as she decided what she wanted to tell him.

"He deserved to die."

"Nobody deserves to die."

"He did."

"What did he do Carol?"

"He raped me," she screamed at him. She struggled to regain her composure and was angry with herself for letting that piece of information slip.

"How old were you when this happened?"

"Does it matter?" she asked as she wiped away tears she

41

was ashamed of. The tears were a sign of weakness. She wasn't weak. She refused to be weak.

"No, I guess it doesn't," he said. "You didn't deserve to have that happen to you, no matter how old you were."

"Really?" she asked. "He always told me I deserved it."

"That was his illness talking. He needed to justify his actions to himself. It had nothing to do with you deserving it."

"How the hell would you know?" she shouted. "Were you there?"

"No, I wasn't, and there's no way I could know for sure but, based on my experience, I would say that ..."

"That's such bullshit," she interrupted him. "And I don't need to listen to this crap."

She stormed out and slammed the door behind her.

Confused by her outburst, she walked on unsteady legs towards her parking spot and the relative safety of her car. These sessions were harder than she thought they'd be. Things she thought were dead and buried were crawling out of the woodwork. She didn't know how much longer she'd be able to keep a lid on her past and stop the bodies from tumbling

out of the closet, quite literally.

5

It was Tuesday morning. Jessie's car was already in her parking spot when I pulled in. The lift made me nervous. I took the stairs now whenever I could, but I was too tired to walk up all those flights. Sleep was a luxury I hadn't enjoyed lately.

The lift doors opened slowly. There he was, leaning against the wood-panelled wall. I tried to move away from the door. His claw-like fingers bit into my wrists and pulled me in. I think I screamed. I must have done.

He stood behind me, his arm around my neck. I gripped his arm, tried to pull it away.

"Did you miss me?" he asked, as he held my wrist in his vice-like grip. He slashed it open with his claws. Blood splattered the walls.

The doors opened and I hit the floor.

"Sarah," Jessie called me. "What's wrong honey?"

"Oh, my God, sweetie. You're bleeding," she said, as she grabbed my slashed wrist.

"What did you do to yourself?"

"He did it," I mumbled.

"What are you talking about?" She helped me towards the ladies' bathroom.

The small spotlights shimmered on the marble tiles.

"He did it."

"Who did it?" she asked, as she rinsed my bloody wrist under the tap.

"That thing," I screamed at her.

She dabbed my wrist with a paper towel.

"Gina said he couldn't hurt me."

"Since when do you listen to anything she says?" Jessie swabbed the wound with a wad of toilet paper. "I think there are some bandages in the office," she said, as she examined the wound.

"Gina said he couldn't hurt me." Tears ran down my cheeks. I wiped them away with the hand that Jessie wasn't holding.

"And how would Gina know anything about this?"

"She sensed he was there."

"Gina's always sensing things that aren't there," Jessie said. "It's how she gets attention."

I couldn't say anything. My teeth chattered and my body shivered.

"We need to get some very sweet tea into you." Jessie led me out of the bathroom and into the office kitchen.

Blood seeped through the toilet paper dressing. I couldn't take my eyes off of the red fluid leaking out of my body. I tingled everywhere. It wasn't a pleasant feeling. I was losing all control and I hated every moment of it.

Jessie found some bandages somewhere. I hadn't been paying much attention to what was going on around me.

"The wound doesn't look too deep," she said as she wrapped the crisp, clean bandage around my wrist. "I don't think it'll need stitches."

I nodded my head.

"Drink this." She handed me a mug of hot, sweet herbal tea.

I sniffed and took a sip. I tried to stem the tide of emotions welling up in my throat. The tea made its way to the lump that was stuck in the middle of my oesophagus. The hot, sweet liquid dissolved it and there was no stopping the tears from flowing. Jessie just stood there, drinking her coffee. She didn't say anything: probably didn't know what to say. She let me cry it out. I cried until I had no more tears. I was running on empty.

"So, you're going to see a shrink, right," she said, once I stopped sobbing. It was an instruction, not a question.

"I guess I should, hey?" I looked down at my bandaged wrist. The sight of my own blood seeping through the bandage scared me. My father's death was taking its toll on me. It was time I stood up and faced my problems. If I didn't, I would end up like him and I couldn't let that happen.

"I'll call Michael later today," I said, as I wiped my tear-stained cheeks. "But I think I'd better do some work before I'm fired."

Jessie shrugged and walked out of the kitchen. I took

another sip of my tea and tried not to start crying again. The not crying thing didn't work too well. I was sobbing again by the time I got to my desk. Luckily, I kept a box of tissues on it. I reached for the box only to find it was empty. The son of a bitch who called himself my boss had once again helped himself. Every time he had hay fever my tissues disappeared. If it wasn't tissues, it was the sweets I kept in my drawer. Nothing was sacred.

I must have sworn out loud. Jessie popped her head around the door.

"What has he done this time?" she asked

I picked up the box and held it upside down.

"I think I've got some for you." She went back to her office and came back with a packet of tissues.

"Thanks," I said, between sniffs, and tried to get a tissue out of the small packet.

"That's why I lock everything away when I leave in the afternoon," she said.

I tried to return the packet but she put her hand up and said, "Keep them. I think you need them more than me."

She was right. I was well and truly on an emotional roller-coaster ride to hell.

*

Michael's voicemail pissed me off. I tried to call him several times during the day but all I got was: "Hi, this is Michael. I'm not available right now. Please leave your name and number and I'll get back to you as soon as possible." All very businesslike. I was falling apart and all I got was "leave your name and number." I think I left him about ten messages. Considering I hadn't spoken to him in months I felt the number of messages would convey the amount of trouble I was in.

I'd just left my last message, screaming, "Where are you? Answer your damn phone," when Sally – a co-worker who also knew Michael – walked in.

"Boyfriend pulled another disappearing act?" she asked with a big smile on her face. I wasn't her favourite manager.

And if I hadn't been so preoccupied with getting help, I would have made her work late. She was also having an affair with our boss, Sean. Every time I saw her, the image of her under the desk giving him a blowjob popped into my head. I'd actually caught them in his office a few weeks before. I didn't think Sean's wife would be happy if she knew.

"I can't get hold of Michael," was all I managed to mumble, while I stared at the rather uncooperative phone.

"He's on a trip with his latest," there was a note of triumph in her voice. One of those 'I'm-a-better friend-than-you-are' things. I could quite happily have slapped her. I wondered what Sean's wife would have done to her. The thought of her pulling Sally's hair and scratching out her eyes made me feel better.

"When will he be back?" I clenched my jaw and fists.

"In about a week."

I wanted to cry.

*

Kevin stared at his phone. He thought about calling Sarah, but the thought of facing her after what he'd done seemed an impossible task. He knew Sarah would never understand. His shame would reflect in her eyes. It was a reflection he didn't want to see.

It was late and he was tired. He didn't have the energy to fake a normal conversation. He no longer felt normal.

He could hear Denise and Carol in the shower. They were probably washing each other. If it were any other woman, it would have been a massive turn on. The images in his head were disturbing. He kept imagining what they were doing to each other. The more he thought about it, the more disgusted he felt. To make it worse, he was turned on. There was something terribly wrong with him.

They'd spent the last three nights together. If he'd only done it once, he could have confronted himself in the mirror, but he'd done it again and again. Nobody had forced him. He'd been a willing participant. In fact he'd been eager. He hadn't been pushed over the edge. He'd jumped.

"Hey lover," Denise said, as she sauntered out of the bathroom. Her hair dripped down her naked back. Her wet feet padded on the carpet, leaving footprints as she walked towards him.

"Hey." It was a feeble response. His thoughts overwhelmed him.

"Are you still feeling weird?"

"I'm okay," he said it a touch too loudly. He tried to say it with a conviction he didn't feel.

"Look, you've got nothing to feel weird about," she said with her hands on her hips. "You didn't do anything you need to feel ashamed of. Okay?"

"Okay," he said, trying to meet her eyes, thankful that she wasn't making him feel less of a man.

"You know what?" she asked, as she crawled across the bed to him.

"What?"

"We're having an adventure. We're pushing the envelope." She smiled up at him as she snuggled up.

"Ja, I guess. It's just a very kinky adventure."

"Exactly," she grinned. "And what's life without a bit of kink?"

"Boring?" he asked.

"Precisely."

Carol walked out of the bathroom, thankfully with a towel wrapped around her. She combed her wet hair.

"Is he still feeling weird?" Carol addressed Denise with an exasperated look on her face.

"I'm fine, damn it," he said.

"Good." Carol perched herself on the edge of the bed. "Because Denise really likes you and it would be a shame if we had to find someone else to play with."

He didn't know what to say. This wasn't the sister he knew and loved who sat in front of him. He'd never seen her as the kinky type. He'd discovered a whole new side to her. It was a side he wasn't sure he liked.

*

The memory came hard and fast. It felt like one of those horrible migraines his mother always bitched about.

When Carol was four, and he was six, he still called her Carrie. He couldn't remember why he stopped calling her by that childhood nickname. Somewhere along the line Carrie stopped being Carrie and turned into Carol. She somehow stopped being his little sister and turned into a stranger who happened to live under the same roof. But in those days when they'd spent time playing in their backyard, they'd been close and she was still Carrie. He'd almost forgotten how close they'd once been.

He remembered the day they built Their Fort out of old logs they'd found lying around.

It had been a cold winter and the air was crisp. The fort was little more than a small box that they crawled into. They sat inside the box with their knees curled against their chests and their chins tucked in. Carrie suggested that they use the fort as a cover while they dug their way down to China. He'd warned her that digging that far could be dangerous and would be a lot of work. She'd giggled and told him not to be silly. She wasn't afraid because she knew he would protect her from all the baddies.

That was the year that Uncle Martin moved in. That was the year everything changed. He tried to forget about good old Uncle Martin. He'd done a decent job of forgetting, but things had changed and memories he thought were gone forever were sneaking up on him and smacking him on the back of his head, just the way Uncle Martin used to.

*

Carol felt invigorated after the shower. It had helped to push away the memories that started to surface, thanks to her weekly sessions. Dr. Brink being away with his lover was the best news Carol had received in a very long time. He gave her the number of an associate, a woman, whom she could call if she needed to talk to somebody while he was away.

There was no way she would make that call.

Kevin stared at her with a strange look on his face. It was

somewhere between sad, bordering on tears, and something she couldn't quite put her finger on. It wasn't hate but there was anger in that look. There was even a hint of disappointment. She wasn't sure how it made her feel.

Denise stood up and Carol marvelled at her naked beauty. Denise took her breath away, she always had. Denise was her soul mate. They recognised something in each other on the first day of high school and they'd been inseparable ever since. Nothing could break them up. Her mother had tried for years and she thought she would finally succeed by setting up Kevin and Denise. Carol had news for her. Her mother was in for a shock. Hopefully, it would give that ice block she called a heart, a big enough blow that the bitch would keel over and die. However, before that could happen, she and Denise had to take care of a few more things.

She stood up, dropped her towel, walked over to where Denise stood and kissed her softly. Her lips were soft and sweet.

"Ah, man," Kevin groaned. "Do you have to do that?"

She ignored him. So did Denise.

The door slammed. They stopped kissing and caressing each other long enough to see that Kevin had stormed out of the room. They laughed.

"He's so easy," Denise mumbled between kisses. "This is almost too easy."

6

The sunset was beautiful. I almost forgot that my friendly neighbourhood shrink had deserted me. I needed to concentrate on the heavy traffic that stood between me and the sanctuary of home. But home hadn't been that safe and I didn't have anywhere else to go.

Traffic was moving slowly on William Nicol; it always did at that time of day. Everybody rushed home to get to their loved ones, people who cared about them. Was there anybody like that in my life? I had friends, but they could manage without me and they couldn't help me now. My family? We didn't get along: my sister wanted to run my life and my mother was as absent from mine as she was from her own. I was alone. I guess I always had been. Some families grow stronger when trouble hits. Not mine. There'd never been a time that I could remember when the family wasn't in one sort of crisis or another. We all got through those times in our own way, but never as a united family.

The sun met the horizon, making its nightly goodbye to Johannesburg. A sliver of a moon was making its appearance as I turned onto Beyers Naudé, leaving Cresta shopping centre, buzzing with shoppers, behind me. The Palace Chinese restaurant was alluring. Maybe I'd give Mr Delivery a call tonight. They fed me better than I could.

Street lights started to pop on over my head by the time I turned into Wilson Street. Just a few more blocks and I would be home. Safe and sound.

The bandage Jessie wrapped around my wrist was making my skin itch. The moment I got home the bloody thing was coming off.

He stood in the middle of the road. His yellow eyes shone in the dark. I slammed on my brakes and swerved to the right. He laughed. It was more of a demonic cackle. Pure evil. Shivers flew up and down my spine. I tried to get the car back into the left-hand lane. All I heard was his laughter. The steering wheel pulled to the left and I was driving on the tree-lined pavement. I screamed as I headed towards a tree. I crossed my arms over my face as I ploughed headlong into it. I heard the crunch of metal on wood. The windscreen shattered over me and my forehead hit the steering wheel.

*

I woke up to the sound of a car hooting.

My body ached everywhere. I looked up. It was dark. Bright headlights blinded me. A car swerved passed me, only narrowly missing me. A man yelled out of his window, "Stupid woman" and carried on driving. I was in the middle of the road. There wasn't a tree in front of my car and my windscreen was where it was supposed to be. But my head told me a sledgehammer had beaten me black and blue. Another driver, eager to get home, hooted as he tore passed.

The car engine was still running. The gear lever was in neutral. I put it into first, and pulled off. The steering wheel didn't argue as I turned into the left lane. Five minutes later I was home.

The gate squealed open. It still hadn't been oiled. Yapping, overweight fox terriers chased after me as I drove up the driveway. Thankfully the barking stopped when I entered my small garden, separated by a plank of wood that was supposed to be a gate.

I dumped my bag on the couch and switched on the light.

My wrist burned and itched. I pulled at the knot tying the bandage. It took a few tries before it came off. I had to use my teeth to get it undone. The dirty bandage fell to the floor.

The wound was gone. It was impossible. No blood. No slash mark. No nothing. Only bare, unblemished skin.

With shaky fingers I dialled Jessie's number.

She sounded sick and stuffy-nosed when she answered.

"It's gone," I whispered.

"Sarah, is that you?" She coughed.

"Jessie, it's gone."

"What are you talking about?"

"The cut on my wrist. It's gone."

"What cut?"

"The one from this morning."

"What are you talking about?" She sounded bored and confused.

"The cut on my wrist, from this morning, which you bandaged." I was frightened and angry.

"Sarah, I wasn't at work today."

The phone fell to the floor. I vaguely heard Jessie calling my name. I sank back into the couch. Why? Why was this happening to me? I didn't understand. Why was he doing this to me? The walls started closing in on me. The room grew smaller and smaller. My vision blurred and then the darkness took over.

*

Every waking moment became a haze of confusion. Kevin didn't know which way was up anymore. His feelings for Denise were obsessive. He didn't recognise himself. He prided himself on being the one that the girls chased after. He never chased them. It was his cardinal rule. He'd learned his lesson in high school.

But there was something about Denise. He didn't know what it was. There was just something about her. He couldn't stop thinking about her. She was in his mind, in his blood and under his skin. He could feel her presence everywhere he went. He was under her spell. He was quite literally screwed and there was nothing he could do about it. He was powerless. It was the first time in his life that he'd felt that way and he wasn't too sure how he felt about it.

He'd read the same sentence about ten times without taking a word in. He was supposed to be going over the sales documents for the new stock of printers they'd brought in, but his mind was not on his work. He hadn't made a single sale since he'd started the roller-coaster ride with Denise and, if he didn't make one soon, his boss would start asking questions. His pay cheque would also take a serious knock.

He was falling apart and it didn't make sense.

There were two women in his bed – most guys' fantasy – and he was a mess. Sarah was a separate problem and not one he really had to worry about. He would deal with her when he had to. Carol, on the other hand, was another issue. He tried to remove his sister from the equation in his thoughts. Carol was not on the joyride with him and Denise, as far as he was concerned, but he wasn't sure if that was how Denise saw it. They'd been lovers for a while and, unfortunately, whenever he thought of Denise, Carol was there in the shadows, lurking, waiting to jump out at him. He kept seeing them kissing and fondling each other.

He snapped a pencil in half without realising it. He'd imagined them together on his bed without him. They were laughing at him.

"Anderson." His sales manager, Richard, stood behind him. "Are you okay?"

"Yes." Kevin turned around. "I'm fine."

"So I guess the pencil deserved it," Richard said, with a sarcastic smile.

"It had it coming," Kevin said with a fake smile plastered on his face.

Richard shook his head as he walked away.

"Nosy bastard," Kevin said, under his breath, once Richard was out of earshot and stared at the two pieces of pencil he still gripped in his hands. There were two things he could do, either he let it all go and just went with the flow, surrendered himself to it, or he put up a fight. No matter which way he looked at it, his relationship with Carol would never be the same and he couldn't turn back. He'd changed. Into what, he wasn't sure.

*

His hand covered her mouth. He'd woken her up. She'd been dreaming about riding a white pony. She couldn't understand why he'd woken her up or why his hand was on her mouth. She hoped he had a special treat for her. He always brought her special treats when he came to visit, but he'd already given her a treat earlier that day. He'd brought each of them lucky packets and then he'd put a Bar-One chocolate in her pocket when no one was looking.

He was heavy. She felt as though he was crushing her.

He pushed her nightie up over her thighs. She was confused. His hand was hurting her and she couldn't breathe.

Carol woke up screaming. Denise was holding her against her chest and making shushing sounds. Her heart was beating fast. Tears streamed down Carol's face.

"Its okay sweetie," Denise whispered. "Just let it out. He can't hurt you any more."

Loud sobs escaped from between her shivering lips.

"I know," Carol whispered between sobs. "Thanks to you, he'll never hurt anybody again."

"And nobody else will ever hurt you like that again." Denise kissed her forehead. "I promise."

The tears came easily, healing the old scars that had recently been picked at. She was safe and those that had been responsible for the pain she had endured would pay for it, just as her uncle had.

7

There was a loud, repetitive banging. At first I thought it was my head banging against the wall. As I pulled my head off the couch, a little on the slow side, I realised that the banging was coming from someone incessantly hitting my front door. It took a few seconds to realise that I was supposed to get up and open it. It took a further few seconds for that information to penetrate my body and for it to obey. I got up with difficulty. Every inch of my body rejected the idea of movement.

"I know you're in there," BANG BANG BANG. "Open the bloody door, Sarah," Tanya, my sister, yelled. Her knocking was insistent. I opened the door to find her with a disapproving scowl on her face and one of her kids perched on her hip. Spittle ran down her youngest son's chin. Slime-green snot oozed over his trembling upper lip.

I was still seeing stars from getting off the couch too quickly for my body and mind, when I noticed there was something decidedly wrong with Tanya's face.

"Your boss has been calling for the last hour."

I knew she was talking to me and I was supposed to respond but her face distracted me. There was something wrong with it, but I couldn't put my finger on it.

"Sarah, you're over two hours late for work."

Justin, her eight-month-old, screamed. As he screamed, his face became a grisly mask. The snot turned into blood and his skin turned grey.

"Sarah, are you listening to me?"

Tanya's face kept changing. It looked like a crazy plastic surgeon had taken hold of her and left all of his tools sticking between her skin and facial bones. They were all at different angles. She looked like a human Picasso.

I couldn't move.

"He's been trying to call you on your cell for an hour but you're not picking up."

The world spun too quickly. It spun out of control. Nausea welled up bringing the taste of bile into my mouth. I tried to get away from them. Tanya grabbed my arm. I pulled away and threw up all over my red roses.

Justin screamed louder. I threw up again. Tanya rocked Justin and watched as I purged once more. The roses would never be the same again.

A phone rang somewhere. It could have been at the other end of the world. Justin's screaming faded into a haze that enveloped me.

"That's probably your boss again," her voice was faint. "I'll tell him you're indisposed." And she was gone. Just me and the roses. I dropped to my knees. The tiles were hard and cold. I was still wearing the skirt I'd worn to work the day before. The edge of the tiles dug into my bare skin. I vomited again. This time the roses were spared but the Lamb's Ears ground cover took the full brunt of it.

I heard cackling. The kind of laughter you only hear in a bad production of Macbeth. I managed, somehow, to turn my head without losing consciousness. There the bastard was. Just sitting there. His feet propped up on the outside table. He wore a black leather biker jacket, jeans and a pair of black leather boots. His boots tap tapped against each other. If I'd had the energy, I'd have had the guts to kill him. But I couldn't stand, let alone rush at him and strangle him.

He stood over me, laughing. It was belly laughter.

"As if," his voice was harsh and grating. "But at least you're amusing. I think I'll keep you."

*

I called Sean once I managed to drag myself back inside. I decided the best course of action was some time off. I was obviously not handling my father's death.

The hallucinations were brought on by grief. That was all there was to it. I needed to take compassionate leave. And since my shrink had deserted me, this was the best possible cure. A couple of days off, maybe a week and I'd be back to being sane. As sane as I could possibly be. A couple of days of chilling at home, sleeping late and just relaxing would do me the world of good. I'd be back to normal in no time.

Sally answered the phone. There was a certain amount of glee in her voice when she told me he'd been waiting for my call. I was in trouble. Big trouble.

"Sarah, you had better be standing outside my office right now."

No 'Hello Sarah. How are you doing?' Nope. None of that.

"I don't think I'll be coming in today," I tried to make my voice sound worse than I felt. I didn't think it was possible to do that, but I tried.

"Then you had better be dying."

"I think I might be."

"Very funny. I expect to see you tomorrow morning with a better explanation than I think I'm dying."

"I think I need to take a week off."

"WHAT?" I had to hold the phone away from my ear. I'd never heard him shout before. Not at me, anyway. Most of the time I tried hard not to antagonise him. This usually meant working sixteen-hour days, with no overtime pay.

"I have plenty of leave and I haven't taken my compassionate leave yet."

"I don't care if you have plenty of leave."

"I haven't taken leave in over three years."

"I don't care. You will be in this office tomorrow morning at six."

"I think I might be having a nervous breakdown."

"First you're dying and now you're having a nervous breakdown." He took a deep breath. "Make up your mind."

"My point exactly."

"What is going on with you?"

"Besides the fact that my father committed suicide, well, that's what I need the week to find out."

"You know what, take two."

"Really?" I was in shock. And I needed to hurl again. My stomach was doing gymnastics.

"Yeah. I don't want a nut case around here anyway." The phone slammed down in my ear.

I just made it to the toilet in time. The seat hit the porcelain cistern as the little bit of liquid that was left in my body shot out.

I sat on the floor. The room spun around me. If I'd been in bed I'd have put one foot over the edge to anchor myself. All I wanted was a sip of water, but the tap was out of reach. My cell phone beeped, letting me know that I had messages. I looked up at the mirror and remembered that a few nights before a bloody message had been left there for me.

"What the hell does SOON mean?" I asked in a hoarse whisper.

*

Kevin sat on the couch, a beer in one hand and Denise's hand in the other while they watched a DVD. Denise's other hand was holding Carol's. It pissed him off that his sister was always there. Didn't she get it that she was the third wheel? He'd had enough of this crap and it was time for him to do something about it.

"Carol," he said standing up. "Can I speak to you in the kitchen?"

"Sure," Carol said. She first gave Denise a whopper of a kiss and then stood up.

Kevin glared at her. If looks could kill, his sister would have been crisply fried bacon.

"Is something wrong?" Denise asked, looking from one to the other.

"Everything's fine," he said giving Carol a get-your-arse-moving look. "I just need to discuss something with my sister."

"He probably wants to plan a surprise for you," Carol said and winked at Denise. She then turned and made her way through the lounge, into the small kitchen.

Kevin followed her in silence. Carol leaned against the kitchen counter in stony silence. Kevin wasn't sure how to begin.

"What is your problem?" Carol asked, before Kevin figured out how to start.

"You are my problem," he said. "Don't you get it?"

"Get what?"

"That you're not wanted."

"Not wanted?" Her voice was quiet, always a dangerous sign. "I'm not wanted?"

"Ja." He crossed his arms over his chest.

"You're the one who doesn't get it." Then she laughed. Her laughter stung.

"What's so funny?"

"You are." She stopped laughing. "You're an experiment. She wants to see how far she can push you, how far she can get you to go, how much she can twist and pervert you. I'd say her experiment is working pretty well, wouldn't you?" Then she smiled.

He hated that condescending smile she adopted whenever she proved she was smarter than he was.

"You're lying." It was all he could think to say.

"If you want to believe that she feels something for you, then you do that. But if you think I'm the third wheel, think again." She took a breath. "Look, Kev. I love you, but Denise and I have a history: a bond which you cannot understand. I'm sorry to say this, but you're stuck with me until Denise tells me otherwise and, unfortunately, I'm stuck with you until Denise decides otherwise. So you need to decide what you want. Are you prepared to do this threesome thing until Denise gets bored with it, or do you want to carry on having a twosome with Sarah?" She walked passed him and left the kitchen.

There was a void where his stomach was supposed to be. He couldn't just be an experiment to her. There had to be more between them. He felt it in her kiss and in her touch. Carol was wrong. She was jealous. That was all there was to it. Denise wanted him as much as he wanted her. He could never go back to an empty relationship like the one he had with Sarah. He stuck out his chest, felt his nuts. Everything was cool. He was the man and could handle the situation.

He walked into the lounge to find Carol and Denise making out. He took a deep breath, felt his nuts once more and then sat down on the couch next to them. He could handle it.

*

Carol felt the couch move as Kevin sat down. She kissed Denise harder and more passionately, driving her point home. What she and Denise had was the real thing. Kevin was a fool if he thought otherwise. Kevin had always been a fool, especially when it came to women. He should have stuck with Sarah, but he always had a habit of biting off more than he could chew; this time around it would be his downfall.

She remembered the first girl Kevin had set his sights on in high school. She was one of those model types. The most popular girl in their school and Kevin had decided that she was going to be his girlfriend. She was also a few grades higher than he was. He went through an older woman phase. Kevin had declared his love publicly and had his heart crushed.

The following year he'd set his sights on one of the teachers. She was a long-legged blonde who liked wearing low-cut tops and taught English. All the boys had been in love with Miss Nielson. Carol had also had a crush on her. But Kevin hadn't been content with only having a schoolboy crush: he'd asked Miss Nielson out. He claimed that he lost his virginity to her. He was gutted when she announced her engagement to another man a few weeks after their supposed date.

Then there was the stripper. That had been one of the more amusing episodes in Kevin's schoolboy fantasies. Her pimp threw him out of the strip club. He didn't have enough money to pay for her. He actually thought that she liked him enough to sleep with him for free.

Yes, Kevin was a fool when it came to women and his relationship with Denise would be another blow to his ego. One he would never recover from.

She smothered a laugh.

"What the hell are you so happy about?" Kevin asked. He sounded grumpy, which made her even happier.

"A lot," she said, and smiled.

8

The first day of leave was always the best. Everything felt new. Even the alarm going off wasn't so bad. I'd switch it off, roll over and go back to sleep. But, somehow, that morning was different. The alarm was more aggressive than usual. I also couldn't roll over and go back to sleep. Sleep eluded me. Every bump in the night made me jump. I'd expected my nightmare to come out of the shadows at any moment. Kevin, on the other hand, was scarce. The job normally kept me so occupied that I didn't have time to dwell on his absence. Being at home with nothing to do except contemplate my navel meant I also had time to think about my father. Thinking wasn't necessarily what I wanted to do.

I wondered if taking the time off had been such a good idea after all.

I hadn't spoken to Kevin for a couple of days. With everything that had happened, I needed some reassurance that he was there. That he cared. My phone looked rather inviting. I glanced at the alarm clock. It was a little too early to call him. But I needed him. I needed to hear his voice. Need won over caution.

"This had better be good." His voice was groggy and annoyed.

"I miss you." My voice sounded small.

"You called me at half-past five in the morning to tell me you miss me?"

"Uh-huh."

"And you couldn't wait just a couple of hours?" He sounded irritated.

"I'm sorry. I'll call you later." I put the phone down before he could say anything else. I didn't want to break down in tears while he was on the line. That would have been too humiliating for words.

I cuddled into my pillow and burst into tears.

Fingers played with my hair. It felt good. My mother used to sit with me and play with my hair when I was a little girl.

Whenever I was teased at school she'd come into my room and make me feel better. She'd make it okay.

"He's not worth it." It was a husky growl.

I rolled over to see him lying next to me on my bed, propped up on pillows. I jumped off the bed and scuttled into the corner of the room, still hugging my pillow. My heart pumped and I breathed hard.

"Leave me alone," I screamed. I screamed till my voice was hoarse. He laughed.

"Why are you doing this to me?" I whispered, between sobs.

He just carried on laughing as he faded away. Leaving me curled up in the corner, sobbing on the cold floor. Pathetic.

Hours passed and felt like days. I managed not to call Kevin for a few hours. I paced a lot. I picked up the phone and then put it down again, admonishing myself for being so weak. My stomach was going crazy when I finally gave in to the urge to call him. I'd managed to hold out until ten o'clock. He didn't answer his phone. It was tempting to hang up and not leave a message, but that would have come across as being stalker-ish. So I left a message begging him to call me. I needed to see him, blah blah blah. Probably came off as being needy, but at that point I didn't care. My pride had flown out of the window along with my sanity.

I tried to read a magazine my sister had lent me. I read the same sentence about ten times and then gave up. Then it was movie time while I waited for him to call back. I had no idea what was going on in the movie. I just stared at the phone. About halfway through the movie, I surrendered. I called again. I couldn't help myself. My heart pounded some more as I listened to it ring. My heart skipped a few beats when he picked up.

"Sarah, I'm a little busy right now." His voice was tight and cold.

"I'm sorry. I just need to see you," I sounded desperate.

"Fine. I'll come over tonight."

"You're not angry with me, are you?"

"I'm just really busy at the moment." He sounded tired.

"Then I'll see you tonight. I'll cook you something really nice." He didn't need to know that Mr. Delivery would be providing the food.

"Whatever. I'll be there at about eight."

I wanted to tell him how much I was looking forward to seeing him, but he was gone before I could say anything else. There was a hollow feeling in the pit of my stomach. I felt weak. But he'd said he would come and that was the most important thing.

*

Patience was never one of my strong suits. Kevin was late and I paced again. The food was cold. By nine the bottle of red wine was almost finished. But I was proud of myself. I'd managed not to call him to find out where he was. By the time the bottle was finished, all self-control had vanished.

He picked up on the first ring. It was the first time he'd done that.

"I'm at your gate, so open up." He put the phone down and I hit the button on the intercom, opening the gate. I didn't quite understand why he didn't use his remote. That's what it was there for.

I put Kelly Clarkson on. The first line of Breakaway blared out at me. I tried to appear nonchalant. I failed, but I did try. I was angry. Appearing blasé when you're angry is not an easy task. I had my back to the door when he came in.

My father always told me that the best form of defence is attack. Kevin had that down to a fine art. He never gave me a chance to get on the attack. The moment I turned around he put me on the defensive.

"What is your problem?" he seethed, his arms crossed in front of his chest.

"Excuse me?"

"Okay, I'll repeat my question slowly so that you can understand me." He looked me up and down. His eyes were cold. "What … is …your … problem?"

"Which problem would you be referring to?" I took a breath. "There's the one where you're a few hours late and then there's the one where you have the audacity to be angry with me for no reason. And then there's your behaviour at the party and how you took another woman's side over mine, and then there's your bloody mother and how you let her treat me, and then there's the little matter of your complete and utter selfishness when you know what I'm going through. How would you feel if your father died and I was nowhere to be seen?" I couldn't believe my own ears. "So which one are you referring to?" I'd actually stood up for myself. I couldn't believe it and from the silence and the look on his face, neither could Kevin.

"You're sexy when you're pissed off." He strutted towards me. The bottle of wine in my blood stream was doing its job. All fight went out of me.

He kissed me and I let him: resistance was futile. Wine will do that. I was drunk and he was sober. He was horny and I needed to feel something other than fear.

My dress was around my feet before I knew what was happening. I could feel his lips on my neck then on my nipples. It was all happening so fast. It was all a bit hazy. I was floating, completely unaware of what was happening. Kevin revelled in it when I was drunk. It didn't matter that I didn't know what was going on, what mattered was that I did all sorts of things to him. He relished it.

The world was spinning again. Kevin breathed hard, sprawled out next to me on the bed. I wasn't sure how we got there.

"You're amazing," he said between breaths.

"What just happened?" I was confused.

"That was amazing," he said, not understanding that I was asking a serious question. There was also no point in repeating it. I turned to look at him. Something wasn't right. Kevin's face was a little too red. I squinted. My eyes didn't want to focus. I drew closer to have a better look. His face was covered in blood. He was also smiling at me.

"Hey, beautiful. What you looking at?" He was playing with my hair as I stared at him. I didn't say anything as I touched his face. My fingers were covered in blood when I looked at them. I didn't know where the blood was coming from. Examining his face, I found deep cuts all over. He sat up and looked at me. His skin started to fall off his face.

"Sarah, are you okay?" He didn't have lips anymore. I could see teeth and gums as he spoke to me. I couldn't say anything. I backed away from him.

"Sarah, what's wrong?" His nose slipped off and all that was left was a hole where his nose should have been.

I heard laughter. I clamped my hands over my ears to make it stop. But it didn't stop. It just got louder. The laughter was in my head. The bastard was in my head. Kevin was looking at me. His face was gone. What had once been handsome was now just a bloody, glutinous mess.

"If you don't snap out of it, I'm leaving." He stood in front of me. I couldn't look at him. I could feel the hysteria welling up. I shut my eyes tightly and kept my hands clamped on my ears. Kevin pulled my arms down.

"Look at me," he shouted.

I shook my head.

"Open your eyes, before I open them for you."

My eyes popped open. His face was back. I touched his cheek with my fingers. No blood on my fingertips.

"Sarah, you're turning into a psycho." He started putting on his clothes.

I watched him without a word. I wanted to beg him to stay with me. I wanted to tell him that I was scared and that I needed him, but nothing came out. I couldn't say anything. I just stared at him as he dressed in a hurry. Before I knew it he was gone. All I was left with was that cold, cruel laughter echoing in my head.

*

Kevin tore out of Sarah's driveway, his heart pumping. He'd hoped that being with her would help him. That maybe she could save him, but she didn't and she couldn't. They were both drowning in their own pools and neither could help the other. He didn't know what she'd wanted from him, but whatever it was, he couldn't give it. He wasn't really sure what he wanted from her. He still enjoyed screwing her. At least he didn't have to share Sarah with his sister. He now understood why Sarah didn't want to share him. He didn't want to share his toys either.

Without even thinking about it, he drove straight to Denise's place. He pulled up at the gate and was about to push the intercom buzzer. His finger hovered over the button. He knew that Carol was there. He'd left them together, just a short while ago, to be with Sarah. His stomach churned. He wanted to be with Denise. He needed to obliterate the memory of the frightened look on Sarah's face. He needed to drive Sarah's madness out of his system, but he couldn't deal with Carol being there. He needed to be alone with Denise.

He could see Denise's lounge window from the gate. The light was on. Pulling his finger away from the buzzer, he got back into his car and drove away. He needed time to think, to figure things out. He drove home in silence. Normally the music would be on full blast, the base pumping through his veins, loud enough to drown out all thought; but tonight he needed to think. He needed to think harder than he had ever done in his life and he could only do that in silence.

He turned into his street in Fourways as his phone started vibrating. Taking it out of his pocket, he wondered who wanted him at that time of night. Denise's name came up on the screen. She never called. Something must have happened. Different scenarios ran through his mind; some good, some not so good.

"Hey," he answered.

"Hey," she said. "Are you still with her?"

"If I was, I wouldn't have answered," he sounded irritated.

"Are you okay?"

"No," he could hardly hear himself. "She's completely lost it."

"Do you want to talk about it?"

"Not really." He sighed. "I think I just need to be alone."

"Are you sure?" she sounded worried. "Don't you want to come over? We can spoil you." He heard Carol's voice in the background, chirping in.

"Not tonight." He couldn't believe he was saying no to her. "Thanks for the offer but I'm twenty seconds from home."

"If you're sure?" The disappointment in her voice was almost enough to crumble his resolve.

"Thanks, but I'll see you tomorrow."

"Ok. I miss you."

"Ja. Me too." He put the phone down before she could say anything else to change his mind. His heart was somewhere in the middle of his churning stomach. He pressed the button on his own remote and the gate for his complex creaked open. Thatched roofs and wooden balconies greeted him as he drove through the complex. He was home. His bed waited for him and a good night of dreamless sleep was all he needed. He would be ready to face the world in the morning.

*

Carol couldn't help but laugh. She had Denise all to herself for the first time in ages.

"So how did he sound?" she asked once Denise put the phone down. She couldn't keep the excitement out of her voice.

"Completely freaked out," Denise said, as she stared at the phone, with a strange look on her face

"Is that a good thing?"

"I'm not sure." Denise plonked down on the bed next to her. "His feelings for Sarah may be deeper than I originally thought."

"But he's screwing you."

"That doesn't mean anything. His concern for her was genuine. You aren't concerned about someone you don't care about."

"So what?"

"She may be able to put a spanner in our little plan."

"That's crap," Carol said, crossing her arms under her naked breasts. "She doesn't stand a chance in hell against you."

"Thanks, but I think you're overestimating my charms."

"That's one thing I'm not doing. I could never overestimate your charms." She leaned over and kissed Denise softly on her nipple. "It's impossible to do that."

Denise giggled. Carol loved the sound of her giggle; it sounded like silver bells tinkling.

"We have Kevin exactly where we want him," Carol mumbled, as she planted kisses all over Denise's naked body.

9

Rain pitter-pattered against the window. Kevin's phone was switched off, probably to avoid a certain psycho. I found that hard to swallow. I could understand that maybe I was being a little needy, but under the circumstances wasn't that understandable? So many questions ran through my mind but still I kept coming up with a total blank. All I had were more questions, driving me even crazier.

I'd locked myself in my bedroom since Kevin had stormed out. I was too afraid of what would happen if I walked through the door. I felt the need to tell Kevin. Maybe if I could speak to him I could make him understand.

I wasn't sure how long I'd been sitting on the bed, hugging my pillow, when the phone started ringing. It took a while for my mind to register that I had to pick it up for the ringing to stop.

I answered in a daze. It took some time to realise that Michael was on the other end of the line.

"Sarah, can you hear me?" his voice was warm and strong. "These damned cell phones," he sounded frustrated. "Sarah, please say something."

I had trouble finding my voice and, instead of words, sobs escaped from my lips.

"It's okay, sweetie. Just let it out. I'm here," his voice was chocolate. Making it all better. I sobbed while he made soothing sounds over the phone. It was one of the best conversations I'd had in a while.

"Do you think you're in a state to drive?" Genuine concern flowed through his words.

"I think so." My voice was soft and small. I sounded like a five-year old who was afraid of the dark.

"I can fit you in for a session this afternoon."

I started sobbing in response. Relief flooded over me as tears flowed down my cheeks. My eyes were red and burning but I felt better than I had in weeks. I was on the way to getting the help I needed. The hardest part about dealing with this was admitting that I needed help. And now I was getting it. I was going to get better. My mind was not going to hold me prisoner any longer. I was going to save myself and Michael was going to help me do it.

*

Benmore Gardens is a shopping centre in Sandton. The offices are not numbered consecutively, so I got lost a few times before I managed to find my way around the maze. I was annoyed by the time I found the passage that was supposed to house Michael's office. It was a few doors down from the Depression and Anxiety Support Group. He volunteered there once a week. Having his office close by saved him time.

The door to the DASG was partly open. I heard voices talking in soothing voices. Someone inside was trying to talk someone else out of killing themselves; trying to convince them that there was a point to all the pain; that there was a reason why they felt all alone; that there was a reason to carry on with it all; that all they needed was to reach out for help. But was reaching out for that so-called help really enough, or were we all just kidding ourselves?

I walked faster, trying to distance myself from the sound of those calming voices and the fear that getting help wasn't going to be enough. I tried to suppress the thought that I was doomed to have this thing haunt me for the rest of time. I heard his laughter again, reverberating off the walls in the narrow passage. Nausea travelled up from my stomach into my throat as I knocked on Michael's door. I tasted bile and fear. A buzzing sound, a click and the door bounced out of its lock. It stood ajar for a few seconds and then Michael's disembodied voice called out, "Sarah, you can come in you know."

I walked in slowly. My legs were heavy, reluctant to move forward. Michael came towards me, gave me bear hug, then held me at arm's length as he looked me over.

"Have a seat," he said after what seemed an eternity and gestured at his well-used brown leather couch.

I sat down and felt the air whoosh out of the couch and my lungs. The whole story just poured out of me. The words tumbled off my tongue. It was a relief to tell everything to somebody who wouldn't be shocked by it, someone who had heard it all before.

At the end of it, Michael jotted something down on a prescription pad.

"We're going to start you off on Resperdal; it's an anti-psychotic. It'll help with the hallucinations."

His face was down while he scribbled on his pad. I wanted him to look at me. I wanted the look on his face to tell me that I wasn't crazy. I only wanted that one look.

"I also want to see you once a week." When he looked up, it was the face of a worried friend looking back at me and not that of an unbiased doctor. I wasn't sure if that was a good thing. Does one ever really want someone close to you knowing, in such intimate detail, just how crazy you really are? Then again, it's the people close to you who care enough to do something to help you.

"I'm sorry about your dad," he said.

Tears once again dribbled their usual path down my cheeks. I didn't even know when I'd started crying. I hadn't cried this much since I'd been in nappies. I wiped my cheeks and managed to look at Michael, trying to cover my embarrassment. I composed myself only to be faced with my nightmare.

He stood behind Michael, grinning at me. His teeth were more yellow with every passing day. I felt the colour drain from my face as he started to make pelvic thrusts in Michael's direction. If it weren't so horrible, I would probably have laughed. He faked an orgasm that would have given Meg Ryan a run for her money. I had to get out of there. The room started to shrink by the second.

"Are you alright?" Michael asked, the concerned doctor and friend. I wondered if he'd seen this coming. Was insanity genetic?

"I'm fine. I just realised that I have to be somewhere." I couldn't tell him what was happening behind him. It was bad enough that I'd told him everything else. Telling him that it was happening in his office was too much for me to handle.

I crossed his office, grabbed the prescription from his hand and dashed out of the door before he had a chance to ask any more questions. I didn't stop running till I reached my car. My breath came in gasps.

I was completely alone. Michael couldn't help me. Looking down at the scribbled prescription, tears rolled down my face and splashed onto the white, crisp sheet of paper.

The feeling of fear grew in the pit of my stomach. I knew the pills Michael wanted me to take wouldn't work. Nothing could help me.

Laughter resounded and it wasn't just inside my head. I looked over at the passenger seat. There he was. He laughed and looked very pleased with himself. As I started the car and drove out of the parking area I saw Michael in my rear-view mirror. He ran after me, trying to flag me down.

As much as I wanted to stop I couldn't. I scrunched the prescription into a little ball; I had to do this on my own. I'd be lost if I didn't win the battle with my mind. If I took the pills, I'd have to take them for the rest of my life. I'd be just as much a slave to the pills as I was to the hallucinations. I refused to live like that. I threw the paper out of the window as I turned into William Nicol and made my way home.

*

Kevin's boss was not happy with him. His phone had been switched off for a few days and sales were suffering because of it. The lie that there was a problem with his battery wasn't working as well as he'd hoped. Richard wasn't buying it.

"Let me guess," Richard said, "all the women you've been screwing around with have finally caught on and they want you dead." He seemed happy with the idea of women trying to track Kevin down and kill him.

"Seriously," Kevin said, "my battery's stuffed and the shop's screwing me around. Apparently they don't have stock and I have to wait for them to order the frigging thing."

"Just get it fixed, or buy another one," Richard said as he crossed his arms and tried to look commanding. "Clients are starting to complain that they can't get hold of you. So sort yourself out."

Kevin watched Richard's retreating back. He was not looking forward to putting his phone back on. He didn't know what kind of messages were waiting for him. He knew there would be some irate ones from Sarah. There would also be a few pathetic, pleading ones from her. Those would annoy the shit out of him. He wondered if there would be any from Denise. He hadn't seen his family or Carol in the last couple of days either. He hoped Denise was worried about him.

He braced himself as he switched it on. A musical tone signalled that it was switched on. He put it down on his desk and waited for another signal telling him he had messages. A few minutes later and there was still no tone signalling messages. There really had to be something wrong with his phone. Maybe the messages weren't coming through. He picked up his phone and dialled his message centre.

"You have no new messages," a woman's voice announced.

He slammed his phone on the table. He didn't know what to think. How could he not have any messages? There had to be some mistake. His phone had been switched off for days. Even if Sarah hadn't left any messages, his clients had to have left some for him. There should have been messages with orders or enquires. It didn't make any sense. What happened to his clients?

The answer soon became clear. He heard one of the other sales guys talking to Mrs Wilsher. She was one of his good clients. He'd worked hard to get her, taken her out for a drink, even flirted with her, and now she was dealing with someone else. He was losing his clients.

His phone started ringing. His heart pounded when he checked the number ID on the screen.

"Hey," he answered.

"Hey," Denise's voice was warm and husky. "I've got the afternoon off and Carol's taken some time off from studying and we were wondering if you wanted to come out and play with us."

He looked around the office before answering. He was

the only one whose phone wasn't ringing with orders from clients.

"Sure. I haven't anything else to do." He was the man. "I'll be right over."

He grabbed his car keys and wallet and flung his jacket over his shoulder. He was already looking forward to having fun with the girls. Even having Carol there didn't bug him so much anymore. Hell, it could even be cool to have them put on a show for him. Wasn't that every straight guy's fantasy? He was going to live out his every twisted fantasy and he was going to enjoy every moment. He had nothing to lose.

*

"He's on his way," Denise said when she put her phone down.

"Told you," Carol said. "He just needed a couple of days to sort himself out and to realise that he wants you more than her. Everything's going according to your plan."

"I guess," Denise said, looking uncertain.

"Hey, what's got into you lately?" Carol asked as she walked over to Denise and put her arm around her shoulders. "You're supposed to be the self-assured one and I'm the insecure one. Remember?"

"Ja." Denise wiped a tear off her cheek. "It's just starting to get to me. I don't know how much longer I can do this."

"Just a little bit longer. We're almost there." Carol turned, faced Denise and held her by the shoulders. "Are you bailing out on me?"

"Never." Denise looked shocked at the thought. "I would never drop you like that. This was my plan, my idea. I could never do that to you."

The intercom buzzed.

"That was fast," Carol said, letting go of Denise's shoulders. "You okay?"

"I'm okay." She took a deep breath, shook her hands out and rolled her head around on her shoulders before she walked over to the intercom handset and pushed the button.

"He must have broken a few land-speed records," Denise said. "You ready?" Denise stared at her with burning eyes.

"As ready as I'm ever going to be."

They both exhaled and prepared themselves for the inevitable.

10

Steven, Tanya's elder son of four, was playing in the garden with the two overweight Jack Russells when I arrived home. I drove through the gate and pressed the button on my remote to close it behind me. Steven was an odd child. According to his nursery school teacher he didn't play with the other children. He preferred playing on his own in a corner. As I drove up the driveway he played like any other four-year-old would. Running around, chasing the dogs and making a lot of noise.

It took me a while to realise that something wasn't right with the picture in front of me. I stopped in the middle of the driveway and watched Steven play. It was a rare sight. But my gut told me something was off. Why wasn't it right for a four-year-old to cavort in the sunshine? Was I too jaded to enjoy the sight of my nephew playing like a normal child?

Something moved in the shadow of the trees. I squinted. I could see something in the shadows. Steven stopped chasing the dogs and ran towards the trees. I got out of the car. The engine was still running. Panic welled up inside me.

I ran after Steven. He stood under the trees, his red shorts standing out like a beacon in the dark. His voice was soft as he whispered into the shadows. I strained my ears to hear what he said. I peered into the darkness. Yellow eyes stared back at me. The eyes I'd come to know so well.

Those evil, cruel eyes were in the shadows with my nephew. I yelled as I ran towards them and scooped Steven up in my arms. Tanya ran out of the house.

"What's wrong? Is Steven alright?" she shouted, as she ran towards me.

Steven's face had surprise stamped all over it. Tanya took him out of my arms and clutched him to her chest. After she'd examined him for cuts and bruises, she turned her enquiring eyes on me.

"What the hell happened?" she asked, her voice quiet. She still held Steven, afraid to put him down. Colour slowly came back to her face.

"There was a man in the garden." I couldn't tell her that it was my phantom stalker.

"Where was he?" She looked around the garden.

"Under the trees. In the shadows." I was so sure that Steven had talked to him.

Tanya walked towards the trees. My heart beat faster and faster. Hammering its way out of my chest.

Steven was on the ground standing next to me. I didn't know how he got there. I didn't see Tanya put him down. Kneeling in front of him I grabbed him by the arms.

"Who was that man, Steven?" I was on the verge of hysteria.

"What man?" Steven asked in his small, little-boy voice. It was the voice of a fat little cherub. A scared little cherub.

"The man you were talking to?" I gripped his arms more tightly.

"Let him go. You're scaring him." Tanya stood behind me. "You're scaring me." She scooped him up into her arms again and then they were gone. I was left standing in the middle of the garden and on the edge of the shadows, as they crept closer and closer towards me, engulfing me.

*

Once again the rain was coming down. I stood in the middle of my small patch of garden at the back of Tanya's property. The rain poured over me. I just stood there. I didn't move. I couldn't move. I was frozen. The rain ran down my face and my arms. It dripped down my hair and my back. The dogs stood at the makeshift wooden gate and barked. Heaven only knew why they were brainless enough to stand in the rain and bark at me. I, at least, had an excuse: I was going crazy. What was theirs, stupidity?

I didn't know how long I stood out there in the rain. When I eventually managed to move inside I was shivering and sopping wet. There wasn't a part of me that was dry. I didn't feel any better and I didn't feel cleansed. All I felt was wet and cold. I also felt rather stupid for thinking that standing in the rain would help make me feel better. It just made me feel even worse. Not only was I losing my mind, I was also feeling sick. I'd gone and caught a cold over and above everything else. What else could happen to me? I asked myself, as I stood under the shower as hot water pounded onto my frozen skin.

I should have known never to ask that question. It always invites more trouble.

More trouble was not something I was equipped to handle. I didn't know how much more I could take.

The intercom buzzed at my front door. I climbed out of the shower. I'd just put shampoo in my hair. I scampered out of the bathroom, trying not to slip on the cold tiles.

"Would you like to join us for dinner?" Tanya's voice crackled over the line.

"I just have to finish my shower and I'll come over." I sneezed as I put the handset back on its cradle. I wasn't looking forward to a lecture. Tanya was worried and the way she showed her concern was by lecturing me. I didn't know if being around people, especially my family, was such a good idea. But I couldn't lock myself up either. I had to face my demons or I might as well kill myself and get it over with.

*

The gate opened the moment he buzzed. They were expecting him and were obviously eager to see him. That was a good sign. He walked up to the front door and found it unlocked. He pushed it open, the door handle slammed against the wall. Music floated on the air from the CD player. There was a black, satin, blindfold on the table in the hallway. One of the girls giggled. A note on the blindfold caught his attention. Picking it up he read, 'Put it on.'

He closed the door with his foot and then blindfolded himself, as he was told to. He waited. Every sound was amplified. The girls whispered somewhere close by. Lips kissed him softly. His belt was undone and he heard his zip being pulled down, agonisingly slowly. Someone grabbed his hands and pulled them behind his back. Metal cuffs clicked into place around his wrists.

He was in heaven. This was the blowjob of his life. She

knew what she was doing. Her mouth and hands worked together. Most women were uncoordinated but she was great. He heard a groan escape from one of the girls. He could only imagine what was happening. Darkness overwhelmed him. He could only hear and feel what she was doing to him. It was driving him crazy. He wanted to touch her. She was doing something incredible with her tongue. He had never met a woman who'd done that to him before.

"Oh, God," he moaned. "You're amazing."

"Really?" Denise's voice whispered in his ear.

Warning bells clanged in his head. Something wasn't right. Denise was supposed to be kneeling on the floor in front of him. His heart plummeted.

The light was bright as the blindfold dropped away from his eyes. He couldn't focus on the woman in front of him. She was still kneeling and her head bobbed in and out as she worked her magic. It felt so good. He didn't care who the woman was. She was sensational. He didn't want her to stop.

"Oh God," he groaned as he came in Carol's mouth.

He looked down at her and she smiled as she wiped her mouth with the back of her hand.

It took him a few seconds to register who she was.

Carol stood up, in all her naked glory. Denise walked around him and kissed her.

"So? Big brother," Carol grinned, "was that as good for you as it was for me?"

His legs turned to jelly. Words couldn't find their way out of his mouth.

"You're my sister." He finally managed to get the words over his tongue.

"So?" Denise asked. "Brothers and sisters have been doing it since the beginning of time. Roman emperors had children with their sisters to keep the bloodline pure."

"But this is wrong. I'm not a frigging Roman emperor."

"No, it's not wrong." Denise ran her fingers around Carol's breasts as she spoke. "You two love each other. This is just another way of expressing that love. You do love your sister, don't you Kevin?"

"Of course I love her. But …"

"If you love her, then what's wrong in expressing that love?" her voice was soft and mesmerising.

"I can't think." Everything she said made sense to him. His conscience was screaming 'Bullshit' while his baser self was saying, 'She's right. There's nothing wrong with it. We love each other. Nobody's being hurt. This is what they both want. Nobody knows about it. Nobody needs to know about it.' A smile crept across his face.

"So, ladies." He smiled. "While I recover … how about you two give me a show?"

*

In a few weeks it would all be over. She and Denise would ride off into the sunset together. More like sail off on Denise's daddy's yacht, but the idea was still pretty much the same thing. They'd started planning it about a year ago.

It had all started with those damn sessions with Dr. Phillips, when all those memories came flooding back. Why couldn't he just have left it alone, but no, he had to go and dig it all up. He had to go and make her remember all those things. All those terrible things. Things no one should be forced to remember, things that no one should have to endure in the first place.

She hated herself then and she hated herself even more for what she'd done with Kevin, but Denise was sure about the plan and she trusted Denise. Denise knew what was best for her. She kept telling herself that. It made it almost bearable to pleasure Kevin the same way she'd pleasured Uncle Martin all those years ago. It was the same way she'd pleasured him a few months earlier, when Denise had put a gun to his head and pulled the trigger.

His shitty little house was a few blocks away from a primary school and across the road from a small park where parents took their children to play. It was supposed to be a safe neighbourhood.

He had binoculars on the window sill, waiting for him to

use to spy on the little girls who played on the swings, while their parents stood guard.

He hadn't been surprised to see them. He'd assumed that her mother had sent them over. She'd always been the dutiful niece and pretended to be happy to see him at family functions. Her mother made sure that she behaved herself and always forced Carol to kiss him on the cheek whenever he came to visit. If she didn't, the punishment was severe. He invited them in and offered coffee. Then he said it. She didn't believe it at first, but then she'd seen the hate in Denise's eyes and the artificial smile plastered on her lips. He really had said it.

"You're not really my type anymore, but for old times' sake I'll let you suck my cock the way you did when you were a dirty little whore."

She smiled the same fake smile as Denise. Then Carol pushed him into one of his filthy, brown chairs.

"You mean like this, Uncle Martin?" she asked, in a little girl voice, with a slight lisp.

Denise stood behind him as Carol got down on her knees in front of him and unzipped his pants. The gun shot was louder than she thought it would be. It gave her a fright. Her heart raced. It was the best feeling in the world.

They locked the door from the inside and climbed out of the window. Uncle Martin had never even thought to ask why they were wearing surgical gloves. The cops hadn't bothered to investigate it properly. They'd swept it under the carpet and called it a suicide.

The real reason they hadn't bothered to investigate was that they'd found a room full of kiddie porn in one of the spare bedrooms. Nobody wanted to know if it was murder or not. He was a child molester who got what he deserved. Case closed.

But the case wasn't closed for Carol. Not by a long shot. It would never be closed.

11

The kitchen was bright and warm. Children's drawings were stuck all over the double-door fridge. Pasta bubbled in a large pot. The boys' laughter drifted down from deep inside the house; the TV blared in the lounge. The Bold and the Beautiful theme music announced my entrance into the main passage that led either to the lounge or up to the bedrooms and the bathroom. The laughter came from the bathroom where the boys enjoyed their bath time. The only child that I'd ever seen Steven play with was Justin. The two boys had a special bond that was rare among most siblings.

Footsteps tapped on the tiles, coming towards me. I held my breath and waited. Tanya emerged out of the darkness of the unlit passage.

"Good, you're here." The smile on her lips didn't reach her eyes. It never did these days. Our father's death had affected her more than she would admit.

"Would you mind making something to go with the spaghetti?"

"Are you sure?" I asked. Surely she knew by now that I didn't cook.

"Don't worry. The sauce is done. You just need to make a salad."

"Oh," I said, "I can do that."

"I should hope so," she said, with a small smile and turned away from me, leaving me in the dark hallway. Her footsteps echoed on the tiles as she walked back towards the laughing boys.

Back in the bright kitchen, I opened the fridge hoping to find something edible. I didn't expect something horrendous. Kobus, Tanya's husband stared back at me. Well, his head did. There was an apple shoved into his mouth. I slammed the fridge door closed. Taking a few deep breaths, I prepared to have another look at the stuffed head.

"Breathe in relaxation, breathe out stress and tension," I repeated to myself under my breath, as I breathed in and out.

Once again I opened the fridge door, but only an inch or

two, and peeked inside. No human head to speak of on any of the shelves. I closed it gently. Resting my head on the cold metal of the door I took a few more deep breaths and steadied my heartbeat. The thought of food made my stomach turn. How was I supposed to make a salad or anything resembling food when every cupboard potentially held a severed head or other such surprises in store for me?

My heart still pounded in my chest. It thumped against it, desperately trying to get out of its cage. Clutching my hands together so that they didn't shake too much, I left the kitchen. The hallway was cold, dark and thankfully quiet. The TV in the lounge had been turned off. All I could hear was the rustle of a newspaper as pages were folded or turned. Taking a few deep breaths, I walked towards the sound of the newspaper. I knew that the chance of having a polite conversation with Kobus was zero, but even the prospect of being ignored by him was vastly more appealing than dealing with the demons inside my head, waiting to jump out of the shadows.

The lounge was brightly lit. Kobus wasn't sitting in his usual place. Newspaper was strewn all over the crème-coloured carpet. The smell of sulphur tickled my nose. I heard gurgling coming from above me. I looked up. Something had been nailed to the ceiling. It looked like a man. Blood started to drip on to the carpet. Tanya would be seriously pissed about the stain on her clean rug. I then recognised what was left of the face. His bulbous nose gave him away. Only Kobus had a nose like that. I tried not to scream. I tried to tell myself that it was just another hallucination. I took a few steps back and tripped on the Persian rug. Landing on my arse, I tried to push backwards with my feet. I needed to get away from the bloody mess that had been Kobus. There was so much blood. Too much blood. Did that all come out of one person's body? Impossible.

I made it out of the lounge without screaming. But what faced me in the hallway was worse than what I'd left behind. I got onto my feet only to slip and fall once again. My hands were covered in what I could only assume was blood. It smelt like blood. It was becoming a familiar smell. A smell

I couldn't escape. Throwing out the anti-psychotics that Michael had given me may have been a premature decision. I needed them badly as I looked around me. There was bloody destruction everywhere. A trail of blood led towards the children's rooms. I wanted to run screaming out of the house. But I didn't. Instead my dark curiosity led me on. I followed the bloody trail into the family room and up the stairs to the bathroom where the children had been laughing and playing only minutes ago.

The door was ajar. The light inside was bright after the darkness in the passage. It took a few seconds for my eyes to adjust. It took a few more seconds for my mind to comprehend what my eyes were seeing. Two little headless bodies floated in the bathtub. The water was a murky red. The white, tiled walls were sprayed with blood. I put my hands over my mouth to smother the scream trying to explode out of my throat.

"Sarah," I heard Tanya calling me. Her voice drifted up the passage.

I shut my eyes and tried to figure out how to tell my sister that her two babies were dead and that her husband was nailed to her ceiling.

"What's wrong with you?" Tanya's voice had an edge to it. She sounded angry. The anger struck me as odd. Surely someone who'd just walked down the passage wouldn't have missed all that blood. I opened my eyes slowly. As my vision cleared, so did the scene. It had been so real.

The bathroom was bright. Boys' clothes were strewn across the floor. The two boys stood in the bath waiting to be picked up and dried off.

"If you're not going to help them out of the bath, get out of my way so I can do it."

I was kneeling on the floor next to the tub. I didn't remember falling to my knees. I turned my head and looked over my shoulder. Tanya stood rigid, hands on her hips, waiting for me to get out of her way. Frustration and disappointment flashed in her eyes.

"I'm sorry. I need to get out of here," I mumbled as I

struggled to get back on to my feet. Blood rushed back into my limbs. I stumbled past her. She said something about dinner. I didn't answer. Putting one foot in front of the other I somehow found my way out of her kitchen and into my own cubicle of a bathroom. I promptly vomited everything out of my system. Strangely, I felt much better. The cold porcelain felt great against my hot skin. Closing my eyes I drifted off, with his laughter echoing in the bathroom.

*

The phone's incessant ringing woke Kevin. Denise and Carol were still fast asleep. Their lithe, naked bodies curled up on either side of him. The ringing was coming from somewhere in the flat, probably the lounge. Sunlight filtered into the room through the closed curtains. Carol stirred in her sleep. He couldn't help wondering how she managed to do so well in her studies when she never went to any of her classes. He looked at Denise and marvelled at how she was able to afford her apartment in an expensive complex when she didn't seem to work. He'd always assumed she was a trust fund baby. There were so many things he didn't know about them. That was also part of the turn on. They were both mysterious and he liked that.

The phone rang again. Kevin ignored it. It was probably Richard and he didn't feel like dealing with the stupid prick. He would deal with him later. He was too busy enjoying the view. Besides, he didn't need that stupid job. He could do far better. Nothing could touch him. Feelings of invincibility stirred in his gut. He was young and strong, with his whole future in front of him. Life was great. He was the man.

Sarah snuck into his thoughts. Something tugged at the edge of his consciousness. Maybe he should give her one more try. If she came to the party it would be great, if not, well then, she could get lost as far as he was concerned. She would learn that he was the Emperor in her life and the crazy bitch better learn to toe the line.

Denise had been right all along. There was nothing wrong

with any of it. Sarah would learn to keep her mouth shut about his relationship with Carol.

Although, he had to admit that she was hot when she was angry, but she would have to learn not to talk back as much as she did. Denise's opinion was the only one that counted. If Sarah wanted to be with him, then she would have to share him with the other two and like it.

She would call, she always did and when the phone rang, he would agree to see her. Then it would all be up to her.

*

Carol heard the phone ring through the fog of her dreams. Uncle Martin looked at her with dead eyes. Blood and bits of brain matter dribbled down what was once the left side of his face. His dick was hard and winked at her.

She sat up in bed. Sweat dribbled down between her breasts. Her breathing was ragged. She hadn't thought about her uncle in months. She hadn't had any nightmares since they'd killed him. She couldn't understand why she was having all these nightmares now. It didn't make sense.

She heard Kevin sigh as he snuggled into Denise's naked body. The innocent look on his face made her smile. Denise rolled her body into his embrace and then adjusted her hips so that they fitted against his groin more snugly. The level of Denise's comfort in Kevin's arms wiped the smile off her face.

Naked, except for a pair of fluffy pink slippers on her feet, Carol strode into the lounge and started looking for her phone. She found it underneath one of Kevin's T-shirts and fumed about his inability to pick up after himself, as she looked up the number she wanted. She hit the green 'call' button with a shaking finger.

The phone rang about five times. She was about to disconnect the call when he answered.

"Michael Brink speaking," his voice soft and gentle.

She couldn't find her voice and didn't know what to say. She hadn't thought about what she would say to him.

"Hello," he said. "Is anybody there?"

"Hi, Doc." Her voice was a soft croak.

"Carol?"
"Yes."
"Can I help you, Carol?"
"I hope so."

12

I woke up curled around the base of the toilet. The lines of the tiles were imprinted on my cheek. My stomach made its presence known by forcing me to empty out whatever liquid was left inside me. My life was turning into one big purge fest. A pattern was starting to emerge. Nightmare. Purge. Nightmare. Purge. Nightmare. Purge. It was a little monotonous.

All I could hear was an insistent, demanding knocking. It took a few moments to realise the knocking, echoing around in my head, was actually coming from my front door again. The knocking irritated me.

I struggled to my feet, managed to stand and caught a glimpse of myself in the mirror. It was not a pretty sight. I looked as though I'd been on a hectic drinking binge followed by a few rounds with Mike Tyson. I forced the nausea back down into the pit of my stomach. The knocking grew louder and more insistent. I waddled out of the bathroom still wearing last night's clothes. My vision was blurry. All I could see was a shadow through the frosted glass of the front door. I opened it slowly. Every part of my body ached.

"What the hell is wrong with you?" Tanya's voice was shrill and too loud. I leaned against the door frame. My eyes opened only slightly. The brightness of the light outside was too harsh for my sensitive, puffy eyes.

"You run out of the house without even bothering to explain yourself. And now you look like you visited every she-been in town."

I didn't know what to say to her. I had trouble finding my voice.

"Aren't you supposed to be at work or something?"

"I'm on leave." My voice was husky and my speech slurred.

"My God, you're still drunk."

"I haven't had a drop to drink." The truth was I didn't remember drinking anything.

"Right, like I believe that."

My tongue was thick and I thought I might die of thirst.

"Either get some help or I'll find a way to make you get the help you need. I won't allow you to end up like Daddy. You're scaring my children and I can't have them growing up with a crazy aunt living with them. If you won't do it for yourself, at least do it for those two little boys who love you. We can't deal with another funeral in this family. Please, I'm begging you. Get some help." Tanya had tears in her eyes as she stormed off the small patio in front of my door. She almost broke the makeshift gate on her way out. I closed the door and slid down onto the floor. It was a good thing that I didn't have to go to work.

*

Denise answered Kevin's phone. Why the hell was she answering his phone? I wasn't allowed to answer it.

"Gimme that," I heard Kevin's muffled voice say. "What's up?" His voice was husky and incredibly sexy. I almost forgot I was supposed to be angry. Then jealousy took over.

"Who was that?"

"Nobody. So just don't get all neurotic on me."

"Are you still coming over?" I decided to ignore his comment.

"Was I supposed to?"

"Uh, ja." We were supposed to have gone out for a movie. We'd made plans earlier that day. After I'd managed to drag my arse off the tiles, I'd phoned him and said I needed to get out. The movie was due to start at quarter-past-seven.

"You said you would be here at seven."

"What time is it now?"

"Ten."

"Something came up." I heard laughter in the background. Denise was laughing. Giggling.

"What's going on?"

"Nothing. I'll be over later." That was it. Nothing more. No 'goodbye'. No 'I miss you'. No 'I'll be there in ten minutes'. No 'I'm sorry for being such a wanker.'

I wanted to go to sleep. Sleep through him buzzing at the gate. He would actually have to use his remote for a change.

He only used it to let himself out, but I always had to let him in. I wanted to not be there when he arrived, but I knew I would wait up for him. I would get prettied up for him and every car I heard would be his. I would pace up and down, looking in the mirror every few minutes, making sure I looked perfect for him. I hated myself for clinging to him. He was the only thing I had to cling to. Tears burst out and took my eyeliner with them.

While I waited, scenarios about Denise haunted me. I kept seeing them together. Kissing. Laughing at me. I wondered what he would tell her. I pictured the scene in graphic detail with him holding her and her playing with his hair.

"So who was that?" she'd ask.

"Just this psycho chick I made the mistake of dating." He would smile and she would laugh. "She just doesn't get that we're not actually together. She keeps threatening to kill herself if I leave her." It would be a lie, but she'd believe him. Women always believed him. I did.

She would make commiserating sounds and he would pretend to feel sorry for me.

The picture of them together laughing at me, kept me awake for another hour or so. My stomach kept doing somersaults as I waited. I'd lost track of time when the intercom buzzed. Relief flooded over me. He'd come. He would help me escape the hell I was living in. He would make me feel something other than fear.

*

He was asleep. He always fell asleep after screwing me. All it was, was sex. There had been no emotion or feeling in that so-called act of lovemaking. It left me feeling like nothing more than his whore. I guess I'd pretty much turned myself into that to get any kind of attention from him. I'd become needy. Who wants a needy girlfriend? That's how I justified the new woman in his life. I was needy and insecure. I'd changed. I wasn't the fun, wild woman I'd been a few months before. She was all the things I'd been and probably more.

It was over and had been for a while. It was time I faced up to that. I'd known that it wouldn't last. I hadn't counted on feeling something for him. But were the feelings true or was I simply grabbing for a lifeline? He wasn't going to save me. Nobody could.

"So let's kill the bastard." My heart stopped when I heard the whisper in my ear. He was kneeling next to me, his head resting on the pillow next to mine, yellow eyes shining like marbles in the dimly-lit room. A couple of candles flickered next to the bed and on the dressing table. I'd tried to be romantic. It hadn't worked too well.

"Miss me?" His grin was all sharp, pointy-yellow teeth. There were new bloodstains on them. An image of him biting my neck, blood gushing from his mouth and down his chin, popped into my mind. It made me shiver.

My heart pounded: a familiar feeling. A knife appeared in my hand.

"He's a cheating bastard, who treats you like shit." Yellow eyes sparkled. "He doesn't deserve to live."

I looked down at the knife. It was my carving knife. It should have been in its wooden block with the rest of my kitchen knives.

"Stab him," his voice hissed in my ear. "Just one quick jab and he'll never treat you like a whore again."

His hand enveloped my hand over the handle of the knife. I was on my knees, bending over Kevin's naked chest. I gripped the knife, ready to strike.

"Come on, you can do it."

Tears ran down my face.

"He deserves it."

I told myself that it was another hallucination. Just another bad dream.

"What are you waiting for?"

My heart pounded harder. I could hear my blood pulsing through my ears.

I screamed.

I stabbed.

Kevin woke up.

"What is wrong with you? You crazy bitch."

Blood gushed. The knife was buried in his left shoulder.

He slapped me with his right hand. He slapped me hard. The blow surprised me. I never saw it coming. It wasn't supposed to be real. It was just another hallucination. But it wasn't. Kevin was bleeding and I'd stabbed him. I couldn't move.

"Call an ambulance, you stupid bitch," Kevin screamed.

I was frozen. My body wouldn't move.

Things were hazy and yet strangely clear. I heard pounding at the door. Kevin stumbled off the bed. Blood ran down his arm. Rivers of blood travelled down onto the floor as he stumbled out of the room towards the front door.

I heard Tanya and Kobus tumble into the lounge.

"We heard screaming," Tanya's voice was panicked. "Oh, my God." They would of course have picked that night to hear me scream. Why couldn't they have heard me on all the other nights I'd let out blood-curdling noises?

I couldn't turn around. I couldn't see them. I heard them stumbling in the background of my mind.

"What the fuck?" Kobus only swore when he was in shock.

"The bitch stabbed me."

"Why couldn't you just have stabbed him in the throat," my demon whispered in my ear. "Then we wouldn't have to listen to his whining."

"My God, Sarah." Tanya was next to me. "You need to put some clothes on."

I was kneeling, naked, on the blood-covered bed and I couldn't move. I was frozen. Trapped.

"Sarah." Tanya poked me on the shoulder. "Say something."

"She's probably in shock." Kobus was starting to regain his composure.

"Who gives a shit about her? Would you please call a frigging ambulance and the cops?"

"You really should have killed him." It was an icy whisper. It sent a shiver down my spine. Every other sound faded into the darkness. I was alone: alone in the shadows, with no way out.

*

The painkillers had worn off and his arm throbbed with pain. Denise and Carol both clucked around him. The doctors had sewn him up and said that it wasn't too serious, but that there may be some minor nerve damage. At least he didn't have to stay overnight. The hospital needed the bed for someone with more serious injuries.

He would make the crazy bitch pay for stabbing him. She would never see the light of day again. If she ever did get out he would be waiting, and would make her suffer some more.

"How dare she?" Denise fumed as she paced next to the bed. Kevin wasn't sure who was angrier, him or Denise. Carol sat in the corner, silent, pale and obviously shaken. He was warmed by their love for him. He knew they cared. If they didn't care about him they wouldn't be with him in the hospital. Their reactions spoke volumes. They were his women and his family. The three of them could face the world together.

"She'll pay for this," Denise mumbled as she continued to pace.

"Please stop pacing." It was the first time Carol uttered anything. "You're going to wear a hole in the floor."

"It's just so wrong." Denise's nostrils flared as she huffed. "When I get my hands on that woman ..."

"You don't need to worry your pretty little head about it." Carol stood up and walked towards her. "She'll be charged with attempted murder and they'll lock her up." She put her arm around Denise's shoulders. "She'll get what she deserves."

"How can you be so sure?" Denise sniffed away unshed tears.

"I have faith in the system." Her smile was strange, but he put it down to the fact that she was worried about him.

"And what if your faith is misplaced?" Kevin asked. He felt left out.

"Well," she sighed. "Then we make a plan."

"What kind of plan?" Denise looked up with interest.

"I know a couple of guys who, for a couple of grand, can organise a girl to be gang-raped. They'll dump her somewhere in Soweto. It's worse than dying."

"I don't know what's scarier, the fact that you know people like that, or that you even think like that," Kevin said, looking at his sister with new-found respect.

"I think it's sexy when you think like that," Denise said and planted a hot kiss on Carol's lips.

"Hey, ladies," Kevin said, trying to get their attention. "I'm the one who was stabbed. I'm the one who should be getting some loving."

"Sorry baby," they cooed, cuddled onto the narrow bed and smothered him with kisses.

As they hugged and kissed him, visions of Sarah being raped and left for dead, in some ditch, made him smile. He made a silent promise to himself, she would pay and the girls would help him take his revenge.

*

Carol looked at Kevin lying on the narrow hospital bed, pale and rather pathetic. He didn't look like her tall, strong brother anymore. He was a frightened little boy. The sight of him being injured should have made her feel something for him. Pity or some emotion resembling that, but she didn't. She tried to feel something, but all she felt was loathing. She didn't want to be there. She didn't want to touch him. She didn't want to care about him. She wanted to run away. Put it all behind her and pretend that none of it had ever happened. She wanted to escape the nightmare that was supposed to be her life. But she had no choice and had to play the hand life had dealt her. She tried to focus on the positive in the situation.

She caught Denise's eye as they tried to snuggle on the hospital bed, with Kevin sandwiched between them. Denise's eyes were bright with triumph. She realised that Kevin being stabbed may have put a spanner in her plan to see Dr. Brink, but it worked to her advantage in other areas.

Sarah was out of the picture and Kevin was completely

under Denise's spell. Things couldn't have turned out better, even if she'd planned the stabbing herself. In fact she owed Sarah. Kevin was more pliable thanks to her putting a knife into his shoulder. Things were going better than she could have hoped for. All she had to deal with were the damn nightmares and Kevin. Then everything would be perfect.

"What are you smiling about?" Kevin asked.

"I'm just thinking how sweet retribution can be."

"You are so right," Kevin said. "I'm so glad we're all on the same page."

He sighed.

Carol and Denise giggled.

13

The room was cold and sterile. No curtains on the windows, only plain, grey blinds. The walls were another dirty shade of grey. Everything was grey. I sat in a wheelchair, in front of a window with a view of a garden. The garden had long ago been left to die. Just as I had been left to wither away in the chair. Hours passed like lifetimes. Time didn't seem to matter. Nothing mattered. I was dead to the outside world.

The sounds of the other inmates were distant and muted. Michael had been here, briefly, the day they locked me away. I wasn't even sure when that was. I hadn't seen him since. Everything else was a blur. I didn't know where I was. I could have been in prison for all I knew. It felt like it. All I knew was the wheelchair and the window they put me in front of every morning.

The only thing left from my old life was my own personal demon, my constant companion. He never left my side.

A muffled scream escaped from one of the cells. I pretended not to hear it and stared out of the window. A couple of birds chirped in the dying trees.

As I stared out in front of me, I could see my hands resting on my thighs. I couldn't see my feet or the rest of my body, which had stopped working the night I stabbed Kevin. I was trapped in a broken shell, in a prison of my own making.

My view of the world around me was distorted. I saw everything through the reflection in the window. It made everything around me all the more unreal.

He stood behind me, laughing. Everything around us amused him, especially the screams of the other inmates. The sounds around me were straight out of my nightmares. Nightmares from a time before it all started. I lived in a horror movie and I didn't even get to direct it.

As I stared out of the window, I watched the birds fly away as though a predator were on the move. Then I noticed two men having an argument in the garden. I hadn't noticed them before. One was tall and the other was a head shorter. The taller one seemed to be in control. They were both wearing the hideous grey pyjamas the male inmates were made to wear. I couldn't make out their features, only that they looked similar. The short one was a diminutive version of the other. As I watched, they proceeded to have a heated argument. It looked like a lovers' spat. Their feet crunched long-dead leaves as the short one tried to walk away. The taller one was hazy around the edges. I tried scrunching my eyes closed to refocus and see him clearly. It didn't work. The muscles around my eyes refused to cooperate. He continued to be misty, almost ghost-like.

He grabbed the shorter one by the arm. The short man spun around. With a gun in his hand. He pulled the trigger. The tall one shimmered as the bullet passed through him, but he carried on standing. He even laughed. The short one put the gun to his right temple and pulled the trigger once again. The noise from the shot echoed around in my head. The short man thumped on the ground. The tall one looked triumphant. He smiled as he faded away into nothing.

"Way to go," my demon shouted and clapped his hands. "I know that guy. He's pretty new but he's getting the hang of it." I heard pride in his voice.

The short one remained lying on the ground, his blood nourishing the dead earth.

*

Cells disappeared as I sped down the passage. Legs ran past. Screams echoed. Running feet pounded. Then the silence of my cell, and the sound of the bolt locking into place. I was alone, away from my window and the blood. I only had the smell of disinfectant to keep me company.

Since being locked away I couldn't handle being alone. I missed my demon. I felt as though something was missing whenever he wasn't with me. He was all I had. Without him there was only emptiness and grey walls.

"It's good that you miss me," he whispered in my ear. "I'm the only one who cares about what happens to you."

A part of me believed him, but there was still a part of me that hoped there were still people in my life who truly did love me. Maybe my mother, or even my sister? I thought of Kevin and a startling pain enveloped my heart. I saw him with Denise, cuddling on a couch or holding hands. I pushed the image aside. I didn't want to think about him or what I'd done to him. I could still see the blood and the knife.

"Don't think about that. He deserved it. As for your so-called family, they don't love you," he said from his reclined position on my narrow steel-framed bed. "They haven't been to see you, have they?"

They hadn't. I kept telling myself that there had to be a reason why they'd deserted me. Maybe the people in charge of this place wouldn't let them. Maybe none of this was real. I was probably still lying in bed fast asleep, Kevin snoring. And there was no Denise. This all had to be a terrible dream filled with horrific visions. It was all in my head. It had to be. This couldn't be my life.

"Afraid not, sweetie." He grinned. "This is all very real."

Hallucination or reality, it didn't matter. Either way I was screwed.

*

It was unbelievable. The bitch had got off lightly. The judge had decided that due to her diminished capacity, she would be put in some nut house for observation. They hadn't even charged her with attempted murder. The shyster lawyer her bitch sister and her jerk-off husband had hired, did some tap dance and Sarah got away with stabbing him. He knew she was faking that so-called catatonic state. She was a lying bitch and he would prove it, if it was the last thing he did.

Once he'd exposed her for the fake that she was, he'd then have her gang-raped. He'd already bought a cool digital camera so that he could film it. He wanted to commit her demise to posterity so that he could watch it whenever he wanted.

His shoulder was in a sling and would be for some time. It was a reminder of what that psycho had done to him. The nerve damage had been more severe than the stupid doctors had originally thought and the incompetent physiotherapist wasn't fixing him fast enough. All the guy did was cause him more pain. Every time he tried to move his arm the pain seared his brain, and he thought of Sarah. The anger would bubble out of him all over again. If she stood in front of him now, he would throttle her with his bare hands. He'd lost his job because of her and now he couldn't even enjoy Denise and Carol as much as he wanted to. His shoulder always hurt and the sling got in the way when they were in bed together. It was humiliating. She'd robbed him of his manhood.

He skulked around the flat he shared with the two girls. Since he'd lost his job he couldn't afford to pay his rent, so the girls decided that they should all move in together. As far as his parents were concerned, only he and Denise shared the master bedroom. They were relieved that his involvement with Sarah had come to an end, but they never mentioned the stabbing. They had been proved right about her, which was all that mattered to them.

Denise and Carol left him to rattle around the flat on his own. He hated it when they left him. His skin felt as though it was crawling around on his body. He didn't know what to do with himself. Daytime TV sucked and the painkillers only worked for a couple of hours. As a result, he was taking double the amount indicated on the bottle. Two pills instead of one worked much better. The doctor was an imbecile, anyway. They also worked well if he took them with a beer. When the girls went off together, he took a few pills, drank a few beers and passed out on the couch. Much better. The only problem was that he was starting to run low on pills. He wasn't sure how he was going to explain that to the tight-arsed prick who called himself a doctor.

The pills started to kick in as he took another swig of beer. He stumbled onto the couch.

"I could tell the dumb fuck I lost my pills," he mumbled to himself, as his eyes felt heavier and the room grew darker. "He'll believe me. He'll give me more." The half-finished beer slipped out of his hand and spilt all over the carpet, as he slid into a comatose sleep.

*

"I think things are going rather well," Carol said to Denise over a cup of coffee at the Brazilian in Rosebank. Being alone with Denise was bliss. It was even better knowing that Kevin was in a drunken stupor. Life was great.

"Yes," Denise said, stirring her coffee. "They are going very well."

"You don't sound happy," Carol said, reaching for Denise's hand.

"Don't get me wrong. I'm very pleased with the way things are going, but I'm worried how this may all affect you in time."

"What are you talking about?"

"He's still your brother." She squeezed Carol's hand.

"So what?"

"It doesn't matter what he's done in the past. He will always be your brother and, in a few years to come, you might regret what we've done." Denise stared at her coffee for a few seconds. "I'm also worried that you'll blame me for it all."

"I could never blame you. I love you."

"That could also change."

"What are you trying to say?" She could hear the fear in her voice. "Have your feelings changed?"

"No, they haven't and I very much doubt that they ever will. I love you with all my heart and soul. That's never going to change."

Carol felt tears of relief sting her eyes. The sad look on Denise's face scared her more than any of the nightmares she'd had since she was a child.

"Please stop worrying," Carol said as she wiped a tear from her cheek with the back of her hand. "Kevin deserves everything we have planned for him and more."

"I know he does. What he did to you is unforgivable and he deserves his punishment."

They both sighed and wiped away their tears. Then laughed, as only those who are happy in the knowledge of their own doom can laugh.

14

Dawn light slithered through the small, high window of my cell. I'd been left in the chair all night. The orderlies didn't bother moving me. They wheeled me from my cell to the window in the morning, then collected me when the sun set, only to lock me in my cell again. I never left the chair. They also only changed my catheter when the smell was too bad for them to handle.

Strangely enough, it didn't bother me. Nothing really bothered me anymore. I was removed from it all. It was like watching a movie of someone else's life being acted out in front of me.

Light played on the wall. The bed that I would probably never sleep in was on my right. It didn't matter. I never slept anyway. Thanks to the drugs they fed me intravenously, sleep was simply pure unconsciousness.

What will the in-flight entertainment be? I asked myself.

A key scraped in the lock. The bolt slid out of its nest in the door frame and the door opened. Hands gripped the back of my wheelchair. I was spun around and faced the door. I was once again on my way to the window, my only glimpse of the outside world.

He waited for me at the window. I decided that I had to come up with a name for him. Jason? No, that was just too much of a cliché and he didn't remind me of Freddy Kruger. What about Jack? Jack could work. I decided to name him after one of my father's friends. He was a particularly freaky bugger who gave me the creeps. It was the perfect name, it suited him. I should have named him sooner, but I'd been too distracted by everything else to think about it. Besides, he hadn't exactly been forthcoming in the names department either. If he didn't like the name I'd given him, well, that was his problem. The name Jack was sticking, whether he liked it or not.

There he stood, lit from behind and with a smirk on his face. The orderly put me in the usual spot. I could have sworn that there was a marker on the floor. He always put me in the exact same spot. Jack took up his usual position to the right and a step behind me. He stood there the entire time I was at the window. It was almost as though he was standing guard. I didn't know who he was protecting me from. I only needed protection from him.

"Hello, Sarah," a man's voice said. I couldn't see him. "I'm Dr. Lynche." He came around and sat on his haunches in front of me. He had salt and pepper hair. There was something about his eyes. They reminded me of a cloudy, moonless night.

"Your friend Dr. Brink has asked me to take over your treatment." He smiled. "Apparently, you've been a very bad girl and didn't take the meds he gave you. That was very naughty of you, Sarah."

I wanted to tell him that I wasn't a child and that being a condescending dickhead wasn't going to get me to be cooperative. But I couldn't find my voice.

"This is the guy you need to be protected from," Jack whispered into my ear.

"I'm going to take good care of you, Sarah," Dr. Lynche said, in a soothing voice that doctors reserve for children and old ladies. "We'll begin treatment shortly." He stood up and looked down at me. "It's a shame to see such a beautiful girl wasting away."

I felt a prick on my arm as an injection needle punctured my skin and then everything went hazy and faded into darkness.

*

I lay flat on my back. The overhead light was bright. I didn't know how I'd arrived there. How had they managed to get my legs straight? Dr. Lynche's voice was muffled and seemed far away. Everything was far away, except for the bright light shining into my face.

"We're going to do a direct bilateral ECT today." His voice sounded jovial.

A nurse put something on my temples. They looked like

something out of the old Frankenstein movies. What the hell was an ECT?

"They're going to shock the shit out of you." Jack was back and standing over me. Dr. Lynche came into view and stood on the other side. All I could see were their two faces leering at me. At least they blocked the light.

It happened with out any warning. The jolt was unexpected. Electric current sent shock waves through my body. All I could see, as my body thrashed, was Dr. Lynche's face. He looked as though he was watching an ant under a magnifying glass, as the heat of the sun fried the poor creature.

The convulsions lasted for about a minute but it felt like an hour.

"Now that's what I call entertainment." Jack's laughing face in contrast to Dr. Lynche's serious, studious expression. "I think he should do it again."

My body stopped its puppet dance on the gurney. My feet and hands still twitched. I gasped for air. I felt like a goldfish, trapped in a bowl of dirty water, struggling for air.

I'd only just managed to fill my lungs with air when he zapped me again. I did the crazy puppet dance all over again. I heard something crack. A shot of pain went through the top of my head. The muscles in my face were dancing to a tune of their own. It stopped as suddenly as it started. I heard Jack's laughter over the buzzing in my ear.

"I told you he was the one you needed to worry about." He wasn't laughing any more. He looked worried. Before I could ask him why, everything faded into darkness.

*

The door slammed. Kevin woke up with a start. Denise and Carol were blurred around the edges and staring down at him. A few empty beer bottles were strewn around the couch, on the floor. He wasn't sure how long he'd been asleep. His empty pill bottle lay on the table next to him. Denise picked up the bottle.

"Went through these a bit fast, didn't you?" she asked, as she examined the empty bottle.

"I'm in a lot of pain," he said, sitting up. "I need to take a couple for them to work."

"So what you're saying is that you need something stronger," Carol said, with her arms crossed.

"Ja," he said, not sure where she was heading with the question. He watched the girls exchange looks that he didn't understand. The fog in his mind was taking its time to clear.

"We've got something that'll make you feel better," Denise said, as a smile brightened up her face.

Carol walked behind her and put her hand in Denise's jean pocket. She had a small see-through plastic packet in her hand with white powder in it.

"Is that what I think it is?" Kevin asked, as comprehension dawned.

"That depends on what you think it is," Denise said with a wink.

"If it's what I think it is, I think I love you." Kevin smiled. He hadn't had any snarf in a while. Sarah refused to try it and always made a scene when he wanted to do a line. He'd missed it.

Carol shook out some of the coke onto the glass top of the coffee table. A razor blade appeared out of nowhere in Denise's hand, which divided the cocaine into three lines. Carol rolled up a one-hundred Rand note into a thin pipe and snorted up the first line, before handing the note over to Denise. Denise knelt down at the table and snorted her line. With a grin, she handed the rolled-up note to Kevin. There was something strange about the way she looked at him. It was almost a look of triumph, but he decided he imagined it. He took the note and did his line.

He felt the drug course through his veins. He felt as though he was on top of the world. He was the man; he could do anything.

"We should do something," Denise said, as she edged forwards, her elbows on the coffee table.

"Like what?" Kevin asked

"We could kill someone," Denise said.

*

Killing somebody else had not been something they'd discussed. It wasn't that Carol was against it, but it would have been nice if Denise had let her know what she was planning. She hated not being kept in the loop. Denise was doing that a lot of late, making plans without her; however, she had to admit that persuading Kevin to kill somebody was a stroke of genius.

"Can I see you in the bedroom?" Carol hissed at Denise.

"Sure," Denise said, as she stood up.

"Hey, sis, why don't you have another line and just chill," Kevin said, while still holding the rolled-up note. He sniffed a few times.

"I have an idea, why don't you snort another line and let the adults have a discussion in peace."

"Fine," he said, his eyes beginning to show the effects of the drugs. "I'll cut myself a nice thick line, then."

"Fine," Carol said, as she pulled Denise towards the bathroom. "What the hell is going on with you?" she whispered once they were in the bedroom.

"Oh, come on," Denise sighed. "You have to admit, it's brilliant."

"I'll admit that in principle it's pretty interesting, but killing somebody else was never part of the plan."

"Oh, relax." Denise smiled. "I've already found the perfect person. Nobody will ever miss him. We'll be doing society a favour."

"I'm not sure about this."

"Just trust me," Denise said, as she walked out of the bedroom towards Kevin.

"What's up?" Kevin asked, as Denise sat down next to him on the couch.

"We're going to have a night out on the town," Denise giggled. "It'll be a night we'll never forget."

Carol's heart skipped a beat and then sank to her stomach.

15

Pins and needles prickled my body. My head felt as though it was about to explode. I'd almost forgotten how it felt to have sensation in my limbs. I wasn't sure the feeling was a good thing.

I had trouble thinking and my memory of the previous day was hazy. I knew something had happened. Something I shouldn't be happy about. Something painful. Jack was lying on his back on my bed. At least one of us was getting to lie in a bed.

"So you don't remember what happened yesterday?" he asked, as he stared up at the ceiling, his head resting in the palms of his hands. "I'm sure the good doctor will arrange a reminder for you shortly."

The cell door opened behind me as sunlight stole through the window. Right on time. Another day in hell began. They whisked me passed the other cells. Screams reverberated down the passage. A woman stood against the wall and knocked her forehead, repeatedly, against it. The bloody bandage let me know that she'd done it before. Another woman sat on the floor with her knees against her chest and rocked back and forth, talking to herself. We were at the window again. In the exact same spot.

Shouts and screams continued to drift down the passage towards me. They were sounds I hoped I would never get used to. I hoped they would eventually fade away.

"Hello, Sarah." Dr. Lynche's voice came from behind.

"I think he's going to remind you of what happened yesterday," Jack said. I didn't need to see the smirk on Jack's face. I could hear it in his voice.

Lynche sat on his haunches in front of me. His fingers caressed my ankle.

"It looks like you've hurt yourself, Sarah," his tone was soft and smooth. I didn't know what he was talking about. How could I have hurt myself? I was stuck in a chair with nowhere to go. It wasn't like I could run a marathon or jump off bridges.

As he prodded my ankle, new and painful sensations flooded up my leg. I wanted to yelp like a wounded puppy, but I couldn't get the message from my brain down to my mouth and vocal cords. My ankle was swollen and my foot was at a strange angle. It shouldn't have looked like that. He gave my foot a quick tug and twist. I heard a pop.

"Well, that should fix that," Dr. Lynche said, as he stroked the swollen appendage. His hands slowly worked their way up towards my calves. His touch changed. It no longer felt like the touch of a doctor. He massaged my calf muscle gently and slowly. No man had ever massaged my leg like that, especially not a doctor. Then he stopped, stood up and left me sitting at the window. Confusion spread throughout my body.

Jack stood next to me with his arms crossed. His face was a thundercloud.

*

Rain pelted against the window. The garden turned into a river of mud and lightning split the afternoon sky. It was the right weather for being locked up in the loony bin. I heard footsteps echo on the linoleum floors. Two pairs of footsteps made their way towards me and came to a stop behind my chair. I was wheeled away from the window and taken down a dark passage. It seemed familiar but I couldn't remember if I'd been down that passage. Something wasn't right.

The room was bright in contrast to the dark passage and the light hurt my eyes.

I knew I'd been in that room but couldn't remember what I'd been doing there, or why I would have been there in the first place. It didn't make sense.

"Anything coming back to you, yet?" Jack whispered in my ear.

I saw the gurney in the middle of the room and the strange equipment next to it. Dr. Lynche stood next to the gurney looking at me. Two nurses stood on either side of him. A searing pain travelled from my ankle to the top of my head and I remembered what they'd done to me. I wanted to scream. I wanted to stand up and run for my life. I tried to will my limbs to move, to do something, anything.

The two wardens who'd wheeled me to the torture chamber picked me up and deposited my uncooperative body onto the gurney. Once again Dr. Lynche attached electrodes to my temples. The shock came without warning. Nobody said anything. My body thrashed around as the current travelled up and down. My head bounced from side to side. My vision constricted into a hazy pinhole. Jack laughed as everything faded into darkness once more.

*

Dr. Lynche peered down at me. His face was hazy. My arms and legs were strapped down. I was cold and naked. I couldn't understand why I was naked and strapped to the gurney. My head pounded to its own rhythm; it wasn't a very good one. There was nobody else in the room, at least nobody I could sense.

I felt Dr. Lynche's hands on my inner thighs. He didn't say a word as his hands travelled upwards. His fingers probed inside me. Tears trickled down the sides of my face and into my hair. He bit my nipple. Then he laughed.

I heard a zip being undone. Dr. Lynche grunted. Fingers were once again inside me. Pushing, hard and roughly. He moaned in my ear. And then he came. Spurting his white cum, all over my stomach.

Jack stood in the corner of the room. He had a strange look on his face. He should have been pleased with his handiwork, but he didn't look it. He almost looked sad, but then he seemed to snap out of it and smiled. I heard a zip being closed. Dr. Lynche shoved his tongue into my unreceptive mouth and slithered it around.

"I'll see you soon, Sarah," he said, then turned and walked out the room.

*

They found him lying close to The Zone. He was perfect. His hair hadn't been washed in years. Dirt caked his old face and scraggy beard. Strong body odour assaulted Kevin's nostrils. His heart pumped adrenalin through his body, making him light-headed. Carol and Denise stood guard. The knife was in his hand, just the way Sarah had held it.

"Hurry up," Carol hissed.

The old man breathed heavily in his sleep. All his worldly possessions were in a black plastic bag, which he used as a pillow. Kevin watched him breathe. He enjoyed the sensation of holding someone's life in his hands. He was God and it was intoxicating.

"What's taking you so long?" Denise whispered.

"People will be coming out of the movies anytime now," Carol said.

The alley, where the old man had chosen to fall asleep, was dark and far away from most of the bustle of the shoppers and movie-goers. Nobody took a dark alley in Jo'burg. It would be suicide. Carol was paranoid. Kevin had all the time in the world to enjoy the moment. He wanted to know what Sarah felt when she'd plunged the knife into him.

He took a deep breath. His arm swept down and plunged the knife into the old man's chest. The old man screamed and fought to get up. Kevin put one hand over his mouth and using his body weight, forced him back onto the pavement. He stabbed again and again, not noticing that the old man had stopped struggling. Blood splattered as Kevin drove the knife into his flesh, over and over again.

Carol and Denise pulled him off. His T-shirt and sling were covered in blood. He tasted blood on his lips.

"Jesus, Kevin," Carol said. "What if he had AIDS?"

"What?" Kevin said, the drumming in his ears slowing down so that he could hear what was going on.

"You've got blood everywhere."

"You don't have any cuts or anything like that?" Denise was calm, the exact opposite of his sister.

"I don't think so."

"It's okay." Denise took control. "We'll take the test and we'll know soon enough if the old bastard had AIDS or not." Her voice was matter of fact.

He looked down at the bloody mess that had once been the homeless old man. He didn't know how he felt about what he'd done. He had expected to feel more, to feel something extraordinary. But all he felt was disappointment. He turned and walked away from the corpse, without a backward glance. The girls had to run to catch up with him. One on either side of him, they walked away, hand in hand. As they walked towards his car, he remembered a saying he'd heard a while ago. 'Those who slay together, stay together.'

*

Things were out of control. Killing some poor homeless guy was not what Carol had in mind. Her uncle had deserved to die; the bloody corpse that had once been a man, did not.

"Are you alright?" Denise asked, once Kevin had passed out on the couch.

"No," she almost screamed. "I'm not bloody alright."

"Calm down." Denise gripped Carol's arm. "You'll wake him up."

"I don't care."

"You will if he wakes up."

"That wasn't right."

"It doesn't matter."

"How can you say that?"

"Because we weren't the ones who killed him."

"What?"

"Kevin murdered him." She smiled. "Not you or me."

"What does it matter who killed him?" Tears trickled down Carol's face. "An innocent man is still dead because of us. We might not have wielded the knife, but we may as well have. We pointed Kevin in his direction. We are responsible for that man's death."

"No, we're not." Denise's grip tightened around Carol's arm. "We didn't make him. Kevin did that, all on his own. He could have said no – he chose to pick up that knife and commit murder. Kevin did it all on his own and he will be the one who will be punished for it."

Carol heard the words coming out of Denise's mouth, but she couldn't understand them. All she saw was the blood. All she heard was the sound of the knife being stabbed into flesh, and the sucking sound it made when Kevin pulled it out, again and again.

"Look at me." Denise shook her hard. Her head hit the wall. "You need to get a grip."

"I can't believe we did this."

Denise slapped her. Her cheek stung. Shock waves pulsed through her body as she realised what had just happened. Denise had never hit her before.

"I'm sorry," Denise said, as tears welled up in her eyes. "I'm so sorry, but you weren't listening. I had to slap you. I'm so sorry."

Carol pushed Denise away and turned her back on her.

"Please forgive me," Denise cried.

"I don't know if I can," she whispered.

"You have to." Denise touched Carol's shoulder. "I love you. I'm doing this for you."

"Since when is killing an innocent man a way to show somebody you love them?"

"He wasn't an innocent man."

"How do you know?" she asked, as she turned to face Denise.

"Because I did my homework." She wiped her tears away. "He was a convicted murderer. He's been living on the streets since he got out of jail."

"How do you know all this?"

"Remember Thomas?"

"Who?"

"The guy you called the idiot."

"Oh ja. What about him?"

"Well, he was a very well-informed idiot. Thomas was in the police and he told me about that man. Apparently he butchered his whole family one night with a kitchen knife. He got out on parole a few weeks ago. I thought it was appropriate that he died like that. Don't you?"

"Poetic justice and all that." Carol smiled, all tears and guilt forgotten.

16

I lay on the cold metal gurney and waited. His semen dried and so did my tears. Jack hadn't moved from his spot in the corner. The two wardens came in and unstrapped my arms and legs. They dressed me and then took me back to my cell. Jack left me alone, which was probably a good thing. It gave me time. Time for what, I wasn't sure. I watched the shadows grow longer on the floor, and then there was darkness. I sat alone in the dark. It was strangely comforting.

I told myself that it had all been another one of my hallucinations, but the pain between my legs was real enough. I didn't know what to feel. There was a huge knot where my stomach was supposed to be. I knew I should have some feelings about what happened, but all I felt was numb. Tired and numb.

Someone howled. The zoo seemed to be louder at night, the screams amplified by the darkness. Someone else screamed a little louder. Someone sobbed.

The darkness and the shadows were no longer terrifying. The screams let me know that I wasn't alone in the dark anymore. It was in the light that the real terror waited. I was alone and defenceless in the light. I knew what to expect from the dark.

Jack found his way back. I wasn't sure when he arrived in my dark cell. He sat on my bed with his legs curled up to his chest and rocked like the woman in the passage. If I could have rocked myself, I would probably have sat on the bed with him. Instead, I sat in my wheelchair and stared into the darkness. I waited: waited for darkness to envelope my mind completely, to shut out everything. I waited for the sun to rise. I waited for the next round of nightmares to begin. I waited for it all to end. That was my life in a nutshell. I waited.

*

It was a rainy morning. Not the hard rain like the day before, just a soft, constant drizzle that turned the sunlight grey. It was depressing. It was perfect. I cried.

A thumb wiped away my tears.

"Good morning, Sarah," Dr. Lynche's voice was soft. I cringed as he massaged my shoulders. His fingers felt like claws.

"I hope you slept well." He carried on massaging me. "I slept very well," he sighed, "I'm looking forward to our session today." His fingers stopped prodding my shoulders and then he was gone.

His two barrel-chested wardens came up behind me and wheeled me off. We followed closely on Dr. Lynche's heels. Once again, they took me down the dark passage. No lights were on in the tunnel and I didn't see a light at the end of it. The chamber of horrors loomed up ahead. I wondered whether it was worse knowing what was about to happen, or being completely clueless until he flipped the switch and turned me into an electrical appliance. I decided that knowing was worse.

The room was dark when we went inside. The light went on. Dr. Lynche stood behind me.

"Put her on the gurney," he directed the wardens.

Their hard fingers grabbed my arms and pulled me out of the chair. One of them carried me as though I weighed little more than a small child. They then strapped me down and left the room.

"Alone at last," Dr. Lynche whispered in my ear. "Now, what to do with you, my dear?"

I caught a glimpse of silver in his hands. My heart raced.

"Mmmmm. The things I'm going to do with you," he mumbled as he stared down at me. Sharp silver scissors were in his right hand. A million thoughts rushed through my mind. None of them good. He ran the scissors from my neck, between my breasts and down to the bottom of my grey nightgown. He cut the thin fabric. I felt the cold metal against my skin. Then a sharp pain as he slid the tip of the scissors inside me. His hot, heavy breathing in my ears made my skin crawl.

Pants unzipped and Dr. Lynche was naked from the waist down. He still had on his white doctor's coat. A groan escaped from his mouth. He played with the scissors on my body. He ran the tip down to my thighs and then back up again. I felt the cold steel inside me. He pushed it in and out just hard enough for it to hurt. Jack stood in a corner and watched.

Dr. Lynche shoved his tongue into my mouth. It slithered around and then he bit my lip.

I was frozen. I wasn't there anymore. I watched myself from a distance. I didn't want to be there. I didn't want to feel what he was doing to me.

"I can make it stop, Sarah," Jack whispered in my ear. "You just have to say 'please' and he'll never touch you again."

Dr. Lynche covered my body with his. He nibbled my ear lobe. His hands grabbed my breasts and then he thrust himself inside me. Sharp pain exploded behind my eyes as he grabbed my hair and thrust deeper and deeper into me.

"I can make it stop, Sarah. Just say 'please'."

"Please," I choked the word out. My throat was hoarse from lack of use.

Dr. Lynche stopped. Shock spread across his face.

It all happened so fast. Dr. Lynche went flying across the room and slammed into a cabinet. Surprise plastered his face as glass shattered around him. Jack picked up the electrodes and attached them to Dr. Lynche's temples as he struggled to get back up onto his feet, only to fall back down onto the floor. The current sent his prone body into convulsions. Every part of his body thrashed around like a toy on steroids. It was all over in a matter of minutes. His neck snapped. He lay on the floor, his pants around his ankles, his penis flaccid and wrinkled.

All I felt was the pain between my legs and the humiliation. My only refuge was the thin shell I'd built around my mind. Maybe if I stayed buried, deep within, nothing else could hurt me. No-one would help me anyway. They were all part of what Dr. Lynche had done to me. They all knew what went on and did nothing to stop it. How many other women had he raped? I didn't want to think about it. I wanted it to end. I wanted to be free from all the pain.

Jack was kicking Dr. Lynche, but I didn't think that the bastard felt anything anymore. I hoped that his last moments had been agony. My only regret was that it had been too fast. He should have suffered more.

The door opened and the two wardens came in. I watched them bend over and check his pulse. They didn't notice Jack give him one last kick. They also took no notice of me. They ran out the room. Running feet pounded on the linoleum-covered floor.

A man I didn't recognise came in a few minutes later. The two wardens stayed outside and stood sentry at the door. He wore an expensive suit. Pulling up his trousers at the thigh, he knelt next to Dr. Lynche and felt his pulse. He then looked at me for the first time.

"You fool," he mumbled, shaking his head at Dr. Lynche.

"Get her out of here," he addressed the wardens and cocked his head at me.

The wardens made their way towards me while checking out Dr. Lynche's body. The man in the suit stood next to Dr. Lynche's head and watched the wardens unstrap my arms and legs.

"And for God's sake, put something on her," he said.

I was carried to my chair. They draped the remainder of my nightgown around me, covering my breasts as best they could. I was wheeled back to my cell in a hurry and a new nightgown was put on me. Neither of them would look at me as they dressed me.

I was left in the middle of the room, alone with my bitter, angry thoughts and the knowledge that I was capable of wanting someone to die. It was something I'd never thought I'd feel. But could I take it one step further and kill someone with my own hands? I hoped not. But how far would I go when someone caused me pain? How far would I take revenge? I consoled myself with the thought that Dr. Lynche was a rapist and deserved his fate. I'd simply defended myself. It was my right. Then I remembered Kevin, and what I'd done to him. I was ashamed. But I wasn't ashamed of what I'd let Jack do to Dr. Lynche.

*

The bag of coke sat on the coffee table and winked at Kevin. He could have sworn it did. It was almost as though it was telling him to have another line. It whispered to him. Another line wouldn't hurt. He'd feel better if he had one more. Denise was asleep and Carol was in the shower. They wouldn't know if he had some without them. He was the one who'd done the deed, they'd just watched. He deserved it more than they did. When they were the ones to put the knife into someone, then they could have more than the others.

The cocaine was sparkling white on the glass top. Using Denise's razor blade, he hacked a nice thick line and snorted it. He was disappointed when he messed some on his lip. He licked it off with a hunger he had never known before.

"That was stupid." Carol leaned against the bedroom door frame.

"Don't call me stupid," Kevin said, without turning to look at her.

"I didn't say you were stupid," Carol said as she walked across the room and stood behind him. "Taking drugs just before you're supposed to have a blood test is stupid."

"What blood test?" His memory was hazy.

"Well," she sighed. "Since you went all crazy on us, we need to make sure that you didn't get AIDS from the home-less guy."

"I didn't get anything from him."

"It's better to be safe than sorry."

"This is stupid."

"No, stupid would be to pretend that you didn't get the guy's blood all over you."

"Fine. I'll take the frigging test."

"Good. But now we have to wait for the drugs to get out of your system before we can have the test done, and until we get the results, you aren't touching either one of us."

"What?" He couldn't have heard right.

"That'll teach you to do minimal damage. You didn't need to go berserk."

"What do you know? You haven't stabbed anybody."

"That's what you think." Carol turned and walked away from him, leaving him stunned.

17

Jack lay on the bed, whistling. It was sharp and out of tune. Blood dribbled down the walls of my cell. It ran crimson and thick. The acrid smell woke me up. Jack's whistling gave me a headache.

"Are you finally awake?" he asked and jumped off the bed. "The bastard is dead and it's time we had some fun."

Fun? What the hell was fun? I was in agony and he wanted to enjoy himself at my expense. I didn't think I could handle much more of his idea of fun. But Jack would carry on, and all I could do was hang on. I had to survive, no matter what he threw at me.

My world constricted around me. The floor turned to liquid and I was drowning. The wheelchair weighed me down and I hit rock bottom. I let the fear go and simply surrendered to what Jack and my mind conjured up. Darkness surrounded me. Shimmers of light filtered down from high above, giving a soft dim light. The sound of water dripped and echoed all around. Water surrounded me but, instead of a sandy bottom, there was a hard concrete floor. It took me a few breath-holding moments of panic before I surrendered to the idea of drowning, only to discover that I could breathe. I laughed. All I could do was laugh. Fear-filled laughter tumbled up from my stomach and out of my mouth. It took some time to calm down and then there was the eerie silence that one only hears underwater. I waited for the other shoe to drop and listened.

Somewhere from out of the darkness came a sound I couldn't identify. It sounded like something being dragged along the floor. A shadow moved in the hazy darkness. It moved slowly towards me and into the light. It seemed familiar. The familiarity was frightening. It came closer, but I struggled to make out the features. As it came even closer, I recognised the glazed, dead eyes, the painful grimace. It was my father's disfigured face looking at me from the shadows. I tried to blot out the memory of the way he'd died.

The shotgun had blown off the back of his head. My

mother had tried to get the bloodstains out of the bedroom carpet, but ended up having to replace it. His note consisted of one line, 'I'm sorry'. That was all he wrote. No explanations. I couldn't figure out why he'd used a shotgun. He had a pretty extensive gun collection. He could have used any one of his handguns. They would have done just as good a job, without the mess. His suicide had left us all hurt and confused. My sister was dealing with her pain by seeing a shrink, my mother was trying to find solace in another man's arms and I ended up in a madhouse.

My sister's way had probably been the most constructive method of dealing with the pain. Thanks to twenty-twenty hindsight, I admit that I should have listened to her.

My father stood in front of me; a strange, sad smile played on his thick dead lips.

"I'm sorry," he said. Blood dribbled out of his mouth as he spoke. "I didn't want you to go through this."

Tears ran down my cheeks. I tried to suppress my sobs. I didn't want to give Jack the satisfaction of breaking me even more.

"I thought you were the stronger one." My father's voice was hollow. "I thought you would be able to handle it."

"How am I supposed to handle any of this?" My voice sounded strange in my ears.

He looked down and shook his head.

"I'm so sorry, my child. I had no other choice."

I was sucked through a tunnel. The lights went on. My father was gone and I was in front of the window looking out into the garden.

"That was enough of a family reunion," Jack said. "For now."

*

Memories of my father, long forgotten, drifted in and out of my mind.

My childhood had been a relatively happy one. Like all families, we had our ups and downs. My sister and I had played together. It had been more a case of me trying to keep up with my big sister. My parents had tried to keep me out of her hair but hadn't been very successful. I was the irritating little sister who had crushes on all my sister's guy friends and some of her boyfriends. Luckily, as time went on, I developed a very different taste in men. Our family dynamics also changed somewhere along the line. We stopped being a relatively happy family.

My parents' marriage disintegrated and my father had an affair with his secretary. My mother pretended that it wasn't going on and went out of her way to be friends with the other woman. I found out many years later that she felt it was harder for a woman to cheat on a friend. The affair ended. My mother's theory must have worked.

When I was about five or six, my father would carry me on his shoulders. I would take his cap off his head and put it on top of mine; usually I put it on askew. He always smelt of cherry tobacco from his pipe, which I would take out of his mouth and try to smoke it, just the way he did. I ended up coughing and my father would have a good laugh.

As time went on and I grew up, my father and I had very few memorable moments. I moved out the first chance I could. His affair had damaged the trust I had in him. My mother tried to forgive him, but I never could. I also couldn't understand why my sister didn't have a bigger problem with his infidelity. She shrugged her shoulders and simply said "It takes two." I found that piece of philosophy even harder to swallow.

I hadn't seen or spoken to him in almost a year when my mother called to tell me that he'd taken his shotgun and blown half his head away. I never had the chance to tell him that I loved him and that I was sorry; sorry that I hadn't been able to forgive or understand; sorry that I hadn't been a better daughter; sorry that I hadn't been there for him in his final hours.

A few weeks before he killed himself, he tried to talk to me. I told him that I didn't want to hear it and put the phone down on him. I'd been the petulant, spoilt child who couldn't forgive a parent for making a mistake. Strangely enough I'd always chosen men who cheated and forgave them, but I couldn't forgive my own father.

My father had always been a little different, an eccentric. I'd always thought I'd inherited that from him and hated him for it. Why did I have to get the crazy gene?

I remembered watching him talking to himself a few months before I'd lost my faith in him. He would stand in the garden and have heated arguments with himself. Tanya and I would sit and watch him from one of the windows when she came to visit. We would laugh and think him completely round the bend. Maybe he was crazier than we thought, or maybe he was saner than any of us.

As I stared out of the window, I felt closer to my father than I ever had before. I was also starting to understand why he'd used the shotgun. There was no way he could miss with it. There would be no coming back, no miracle survival. There would be no headlines that read, 'Man survives suicide attempt.' It would be completely and totally final. I found it very tempting to follow his example. Then I remembered the mess he'd left behind. Not just the blood on the bedroom carpet, but the pain and confusion he left us to deal with, and the pure selfishness of it all. I couldn't put my family through that kind of pain again. I wouldn't do that to my mother no matter what the state of our relationship was. It was bad enough that I was stuck in a wheelchair and had lost my mind. I had to find a way back to myself, to my sanity. If I couldn't do it for myself, I at least had to do it for the people who, I hoped, still loved me. A mother's love is supposed to be eternal, isn't it?

The sun was high in the sky and I heard my father saying again, "I thought you were the stronger one."

Why would he have said that?

*

The blood test was relatively painless. Waiting for the results, however, was not. Denise, Carol and Kevin drove to a clinic and took the test together. The results were negative, but they would have to go again in 6 months to be sure that they were

in the clear. Kevin was allowed back in the bedroom on condition he used a condom.

The bond between Carol and Denise had grown stronger
while he was sleeping on the couch. It was a bond he knew
he had to break. He didn't trust them anymore. They could
decide that he wasn't what they wanted. They could replace
him at any time. All they had to do was go to the cops and
tell them about the old man. It would be their word against
his.

He heard them whispering in corners. They kept doing
things together and leaving him out. He felt like the third
wheel and didn't like it. Carol's words kept running wild.
She'd said that he was only an experiment to Denise. He had
to make sure that he was more than that to both of them.
He had to do something to get between them. His survival
depended on his ability to divide and conquer.

He heard them as he sat on the couch drinking another
beer. They were laughing in the kitchen. They were laughing
at him. He heard their whispers punctured by giggles and
laughter. Swigging down some more alcohol, he made his
own plans. They wouldn't know what hit them.

Carol walked out of the kitchen and smiled at him. He
wanted to smash the beer bottle against the table and cut the
smile off her face. The sound of her screaming, the image of
her blood soaking into the carpet, made him grin.

"Are you okay?" Carol asked

"I'm fine," he said, disappointed that it had only been a
daydream. "Why?"

"You had a funny look on your face," she said, as she carried on walking towards the bathroom. "Are you sure you're
okay?" she asked again, as she paused at the bathroom door.

"I'm fine." He slammed the beer bottle onto the coffee
table. "Can't a guy have some peace?"

"I was just asking. Don't have a freaking arse collapse." She
slammed the bathroom door.

"What's gotten into you two?" Denise asked, as she poked
her head out of the kitchen.

He stood up and the beers he'd drunk made their presence

felt. He struggled to keep his balance, but managed to walk to Denise.

"She's been lying to you," he said, trying not to slur his words.

"What are you talking about?" she asked.

"Carol's been sneaking around with somebody else."

"Bullshit."

"It's not bullshit. She's been getting these calls from some chick."

"Really?" Denise crossed her arms. "What's this chick's name?"

He had to think quickly.

"Her name's Carla." It was the first name that popped into his head. "They had a thing a while ago. I think she was Carol's first."

"Really." Denise strode out of the kitchen and marched to the bathroom. She knocked on the closed door.

"All right," Carol's voice was muffled. "I'm almost done."

The toilet flushed followed by the sound of running water and then the door jerked open.

"What?" Carol asked.

"Who's Carla?" Denise asked.

He couldn't understand why she was smiling.

"How should I know?" Carol asked.

"Your brother seems to think you do."

Things weren't going quite the way he'd hoped.

"Really," Carol said, as both women turned to look at him. He was screwed.

"I can explain," he said, taking a few steps back. Putting some distance between himself and them.

"Don't bother," Carol said.

"Are you feeling insecure?" Denise asked. The smile twitched at the side of her mouth, threatening to turn into laughter. He couldn't bear her laughing at him.

"No," he said, trying to sound manly and secure within himself.

"You don't need to feel insecure, but I trust Carol with my

life and nothing you can do will break that trust." She walked towards him. "Do you understand?"

"Yes." He took it as a challenge. They thought they were in the driver's seat, but they would see. He had to be more careful in future, but he would come out on top. They were in for the surprise of their lives.

*

They collapsed laughing on the bed. Kevin had passed out once again on the couch with a beer in his hand.

"Can you believe him?" Carol asked, breathless.

"He's becoming a bit ridiculous," Denise said, between peals of laughter.

"I think the drugs are really starting to affect his judgement."

"I can't believe he thought that his little plan would actually work."

"He's so funny."

"But not funny enough."

"And you know this is just the beginning, right?"

"What do you think he'll try next?"

"Who knows?" Carol sighed. "I don't know what's going on in that drunken haze."

"Now what I would love to know is, who on earth is Carla?"

"The only Carla I know was that hot girl in high school. Remember her?"

"Oh, yes." Denise smiled. "Didn't Kevin go on a date with her?"

"They went out for a few weeks and then she dumped him for some younger guy."

"Didn't she also spread all sorts of stuff about him?"

"Most of it was true."

"Really? Like what?"

"I don't know. I can't remember." Carol rolled over onto her back and watched the ceiling fan going around and around. "I just remember thinking at the time how funny it was watching Kevin trying to convince everybody that she was lying and I knew that she wasn't."

"You never told me that."

"Didn't I?"

"No, you didn't."

"Sorry. I guess it wasn't that important."

"I guess?" Denise sounded hurt. "I just thought we shared everything."

"We do."

"I guess not." Denise pouted.

"Don't be mad," Carol said rolling back onto her side so that she could face Denise. "It was a long time ago."

"Not that long ago."

"There were other more important things going on. Like my mother finding us together. Remember that?"

"Like I could ever forget?" Denise frowned. "That's why I don't get your mother welcoming me into the family with open arms."

"You're the lesser of two evils." Carol smiled. "As far as my mother is concerned, if Kevin is sleeping with you, he can't be sleeping with Sarah and if you're sleeping with Kevin then you can't be sleeping with me."

"Your mother can't be that naive?"

"You'd be surprised." Carol exhaled, tried not to cry, but talking about her mother always made her emotional. "You and I together wouldn't make sense to her; only men and women together, in a monogamous relationship, is something she can understand. Anything else just does not exist for her. Three people sleeping together would be a completely alien concept for her. It's not something she could fathom. It's a sin to her and we're going to hell."

"So she's narrow-minded, not näive."

"That's my darling mother for you."

"What are we going to do about your mother?"

"We'll deal with her, once we've dealt with Kevin."

18

The sun's passage marked my time in hell. I wasn't sure how many days had passed since Dr. Lynche had raped me, or if it had even happened. It could have been yesterday or a week ago. I didn't know. I sat at the window and watched the sun travel slowly across the sky. As I watched the sun, others watched me.

A young boy, probably not older than twelve, was curled up in the corner of the room talking to himself. I couldn't understand his mumblings. He was pale, probably hadn't been outside in a long time. The dark rings under his eyes were purple from lack of sleep. He shivered as he tried to comfort himself. He was staring at me. His stare was unwavering. He didn't even blink. The irises of his eyes were completely black. He just kept staring at me with those soulless eyes.

I became dizzy and my head felt as though it was about to explode.

He stopped shivering and stopped talking to himself. Then he smiled. It was a gruesome sight. His teeth had been filed right down to his gums, all except for his two canines, which were long and sharp.

He pounced. His teeth punctured my throat. I felt him sucking. Jack laughed. My blood flowed out of the wounds into his receptive mouth. He pulled away and licked his lips. Blood dribbled down his chin. He sighed and once again attached himself to my throat like a baby suckling on its mother's nipple. The room spun. Pins and needles pulsed through my body.

"That's enough of that," Jack said.

He pulled the vamp child off me, patted him on his head and then the child was gone, disappearing like mist on a rainy day.

"Don't worry, it won't leave a mark," Jack said and then laughed again. "We wouldn't want the nurses here to start thinking they have vampires in their midst."

I didn't think the nurses would even notice a couple of

puncture marks on my neck. I listened to Jack's laughter, and tried to ignore the tingles pulsing through my limbs. I tried to focus, to think. I needed to figure out how my life had turned out to be so bizarre. How had I ended up imprisoned in an insane asylum, stuck to a wheelchair? Questions kept pounding their way through my mind as his laughter reverberated in my ears.

What was I going to do about Jack? How was I going to handle everything that was happening to me?

My mind ran around in circles, chasing its own tail. How much more could I take? How could I fight for my own sanity? What would it take for me to stand up and say "No more?" Most importantly, why was Jack doing this to me? Or was I doing it all to myself? The questions kept coming. One followed on the heels of another. I couldn't stop them from invading my every thought and every moment. My mind kept ticking over, but no answers came. Only more questions.

*

Jack lay on his back, snoring. I watched him sleep. Still the questions kept coming. They'd been tearing at my brain for hours. I tried to quieten my mind and focus on one question at a time. As they surfaced, one kept coming back to me, over and over again. It was almost a shout. Was I doing this all to myself or was Jack torturing me for his own purposes? I couldn't believe I was doing it to myself. I wasn't that self-destructive, was I?

There was a voice deep inside my being, screaming, telling me that this wasn't my doing. There was a piece to this puzzle that I didn't know yet.

As I watched the rhythmic rise and fall of Jack's chest, my father's words echoed in the silence of my cell. How was any child supposed to be strong enough to handle a parent's suicide? Or was there something else that he'd meant to tell me?

Rain pattered on the roof.

Jack grunted in his sleep and rolled onto his side.

Thunder exploded outside.

A plan formed in my mind. It was only a whisper, a mist of an idea.

I hoped that I was strong enough to handle it and, in my own way, find a way to fight back and to save myself.

There was one thing that I was sure of, though. I'd had enough of playing by Jack's rules.

*

I didn't have long to wait for Jack's next round of entertainment. I prepared myself for the worst. I'd already dealt with severed heads, dead babies, stabbing my boyfriend, being raped and seeing my dead father. What else could he do? Have another vampire bite me?

Jack sat with his legs crossed, his right foot bounced up and down. He looked thoughtful, probably cooking up his next idea of fun. I kept telling myself that no matter what he threw at me I could handle it. I would prove to my father that I was strong. But wasn't he the one who'd checked out of his life? So who the hell was he to tell me that I was weak. I would show him.

A smile broke out on Jack's thin lips. That smile could only mean trouble.

"You go girl. Show Daddy how tough you are," Jack said with a sarcastic smile.

A hand gripped my foot. Flesh hung from its bone and maggots crawled all over the fingers that were starting to decompose. The hand came out of the floor like a zombie reaching out of its grave. It pulled me down.

"Great, what is it this time? Zombies?" I asked Jack, trying to sound as bored as possible as the hand pulled harder on my foot.

"Wait and see," he said, sounding a bit annoyed, which only made me want to smile. It was probably a little early to do a victory dance. I was pulled through the floor before I could gloat. Roots hit my face. My hair got tangled and pulled. I descended faster than the Tower of Terror at Gold Reef City. I refused to scream. I had to be strong. I had to be tough: if I could hold it together for long enough, I might make it.

I hit the ground hard and bounced out of the wheelchair. I landed hard on the muddy ground. My coccyx was bruised and hurt like hell. The light from the hole in the floor, up above, filtered down. I stood in the spotlight, rubbing my sore rear end and waited.

There was movement somewhere in the darkness that surrounded the stage that Jack had set for me. I gritted my teeth. The show would be starting any second. Right on cue, a hand grabbed my hair and pulled. Another hand grabbed my wrist, my ankles. Hundreds of hands grabbed me. Pulling. Pushing. Pinching. Ripping.

I laughed. Softly at first, but it ended up being a full belly laugh, verging on hysterical.

"My God, Jack," I said, as my laughter subsided. "Is this it? Have you been watching too many bad horror movies?"

"What?" Jack sounded shocked. I notched a point to my name on the scoreboard. I decided that I might be doing that victory dance sooner than I thought. The zombies stopped grabbing me and disappeared. Jack and I stood alone in the spotlight.

"First, the vampire thing and, now, zombies. Seriously." I struck the bitchiest pose I could think of. I crossed my arms, stuck out one hip and raised an eyebrow.

"We'll see about that." With that he disappeared. I was back in the sunlit common room with the other loons, sitting at the window in my wheelchair. I thought about doing my little victory dance, but that annoying voice in the back of my head told me that it might not be a good idea to celebrate just yet. A sinking feeling settled in my stomach. Self-doubt crept its nasty way into my head. I wondered if challenging Jack had been such a good idea.

*

His first try might have failed, but Kevin was determined to break them up. He loved his sister, but she was in his way. If they stayed one happy little couple, they would eventually turn on him. He would either end up dead or in jail. Neither scenario appealed to him. Maybe Carol should be the one faced with the two options instead of him.

He still had the knife and an anonymous call to the cops would take care of his problem.

"What are you grinning about?" Denise asked.

She and Carol were sitting on the couch when he walked into the lounge.

"Nothing," he said.

"You looked like the cat that ate the canary," Carol said.

"Can't I be happy to see you?" he asked, trying to wipe the smile off his face.

"I'm still not happy with you for trying to break us up," Carol said. "So, you've got a whole lot of smooth talking to do and a stupid grin isn't going to cut it."

"How can I make it up to you?" Kevin asked, trying to sound sincere.

"How about a foot rub?" Carol said, twiddling her naked toes at him.

"Sure. Why not." He knelt in front of her and rubbed her large feet. He enjoyed digging his thumbs in harder than was necessary.

"Not so hard. Gently," Carol said.

Denise watched him with a strange, knowing smile on her face. He felt as though she could read his mind.

"I have an idea," Denise said, looking down at him. "I think Kevin and I need some alone time."

"What?" Carol looked surprised.

"I think that's a great idea," Kevin said, as he gave Carol's foot another jab with his thumb.

"We're going out for dinner tonight," Denise said, as she smiled at him, but he noticed she winked at Carol. He wasn't sure how to interpret their interaction.

"That's okay," Carol said, too quickly. "I've got studying to do."

"That's settled then," Denise said. "You're taking me out to dinner tonight. Best you think of a great place to take me."

"I already know." He was going to get her on his side no matter what he had to do. "There's this great place in Cresta."

"Don't tell me," Denise said, cocking her eyebrow. "Surprise me."

*

The idea of Denise and Kevin going on a dinner date without her was painful, but she knew it was necessary.

"Are you okay with this?" Denise asked, while Kevin was singing in the shower. His voice grated.

"Not really," she said. "But I'll deal with it."

"I wish you were the one taking me out for dinner."

"Let's be serious." Carol smiled. "You would be the one taking me out for dinner."

"Oh, really?"

"Yes, because you're the one with a rich daddy and a nice trust fund. I'm the poor student who is, thankfully, on holiday."

"True." Denise's smile warmed up the room. "Now, help me figure out what the hell to wear tonight."

They stood in front of the cupboard and stared.

"Knowing Kevin the way I do," Carol said. "I would go with the short black one."

"But I always have to worry about my boobs popping out with that one and it rides up," she said, as she pulled it off its hanger.

"Exactly," Carol said. "He won't be able to concentrate on anything."

19

Blood seeped out of the ground where the inmate had killed himself a few days or weeks before; I wasn't sure of time anymore. It might only have been hours since it happened. The rain pelted down, but the blood wouldn't wash away. It didn't seem to bother any of my fellow inmates; I was the only one affected. It made me remember things I wanted to forget.

I saw the stain in my mother's bedroom, where my father had shot himself. No matter how much she scrubbed, it wouldn't come out.

My parents' bedroom was untidy; it always had been. My mother's knickers and bras were strewn across the floor. She'd never been a stickler for tidiness. It was exactly how I remembered it from my childhood, when everything was as it should be. My father stood in the middle of the room crying. He was a little thicker around his waist than I remembered him. He held a pair of my mother's satin panties in his hands. He just stood there with tears pouring down his face, smelling her panties. I'd never seen him cry. I didn't think he was capable of it.

Then he stood in front of me, holding his shotgun. He put the barrel in his mouth, stretched his arms forward and leaned into the barrel. His thumbs were on the trigger.

"Don't do it, Daddy," I screamed. "Please don't do it. I'm sorry."

He pulled the trigger. The back of his head disappeared in a red cloud. His body fell at my feet. The shotgun landed next to my wheelchair. My mother's satin panties lay on the floor next to what was left of his head. Blood seeped into the satin and stained them red.

"Why did you do it, Daddy?" I asked between sobs.

His blue eyes blinked. Blood gurgled out of his open mouth.

"I'm sorry," he said. Blood splattered out of his mouth as he spoke. "I did it for your mother. To save her."

"Now that's enough of that," Jack's voice came from behind me.

The room and my father disappeared from sight. They were sucked into a bottomless pit.

The rain came down.

Confusion ran wild. More questions surfaced but no answers found their way through the mist.

"This is so much more fun," Jack said. "I was starting to get bored. Weren't you?" He patted me on the head like one would a favourite pet.

"I always did enjoy bringing loved ones together," he sighed. "Besides you were seriously not playing along anymore. I need you to be a little more excited, Sarah. I know that after all the fun we had with Dr. Lynche, everything I do to entertain you may seem a little dull. I know I have to work harder now to keep your interest, but I promise you won't be bored anymore." Jack put his hand to his heart and smiled.

*

My life had turned into a constant nightmare. Jack wouldn't give me a moment's rest. I realised that he was determined that I would share my father's fate, and I was equally determined I would not. I hoped that my will to live was stronger than his will to drive me to suicide. The one question that seemed to be screaming louder than the rest was why was Jack doing this to me? I had a feeling that if I had an answer to that then maybe everything else would make sense.

I promised myself that no matter what Jack did to me, I wouldn't give him the satisfaction of seeing me cry or scream. I wouldn't react, no matter what he did. It was like watching a movie, only this movie was interactive on a completely different scale.

At least he hadn't brought my father back to torment me again with his cryptic messages. I didn't want to see my father like that. I wondered what my mother had to do with the whole saga.

I sat in a dark hole. Rats crawled all over me. If I moved I was bitten. I used this time to think. I ignored the vermin crawling on me and tried to focus my mind. It was one big jumble of confusing thoughts. I tried to disentangle them one thread at a time. Every time I thought I was close to figuring it out, I found another knot and a different thread, with a brand new set of consequences.

I hated rats: creepy little critters. They were in my hair and on my face. They covered every inch of me. Every time I wanted to scream I told myself that I was on Fear Factor and if I made a sound or screamed, I lost the game.

"Ok, rats are boring," Jack said. He stood in the shadows watching. "Let's try something else."

Rats turned into cobras. Big angry cobras slithered all over me. My heart raced. If there was anything I hated more than rats it was snakes. I also wasn't a fan of spiders. I wasn't sure which of them I hated the most, but it was a close race between the three.

"Sarah, you're really starting to irritate me and trust me when I say, you really don't want me to be irritated."

I ignored him, pretended he wasn't there.

'It's just like being on fear factor, it's just like being on fear factor.' I repeated over and over again. If I moved, I lost the game. The stakes were high. If I lost the game I lost my life.

I kept my eyes closed and ignored the snakes' smooth skin as they slithered over my bare skin.

"Sarah, there will be consequences to not playing the game."

I let my thoughts wander. I shut out Jack and his game and just floated somewhere else. Somewhere where Jack couldn't control my environment. I floated up in the clouds. It was peaceful and quiet and so very still. Birds flew silently by. I drifted through clouds that were cool and soft against my flesh.

"Your father was far more fun to play with. It's at times like this that I really miss the old bastard," his voice was hard and angry.

I landed back in my chair with a thump.

"He was a whole lot of fun right up until the moment he put the shotgun in his mouth." Jack was smiling now. "He was a good boy who did what he was told."

I wanted to block my ears, shut out the sound of Jack's voice.

"That's right Sarah. Your father and I were old friends. We go way back. I also knew your mother." His smile was sugary sweet. "In the biblical sense."

"Shut up," I screamed. "Just shut up. It's all lies. Nothing you say is true. None of this is real. You're not real."

"Wrong again, sweetie," Jack said, and cackled like an old witch in another bad horror movie.

*

My mother and sister sat on plastic chairs and stared at me. Tears ran down my mother's cheeks. Tanya held her hand.

I wasn't sure if they were another trick of Jack's. I waited to see how he would use them to torment me.

"She has to come back to us," my mother whispered between sobs.

"Mom," Tanya said. "You heard what Michael said. She may never come out of this."

"I don't care what Michael said," my mother replied, without taking her eyes off me. "I know my little girl. She'll come out of this. I know she will."

"Mom," Tanya's voice was pleading. Her eyes were bloodshot and the dark rings under her eyes were more pronounced since the last time I'd seen her.

"Don't you 'Mom' me. I know my daughter better than some quack who didn't even know the colleague he'd entrusted Sarah to, his friend, was a rapist."

"There's no way Michael could have known that was going to happen to Sarah."

"I don't care," she sobbed. "He should have taken better care of her."

"He tried to, but Sarah wouldn't take the medication he prescribed."

"So, are you trying to tell me that this is Sarah's fault?" Her voice had an edge to it. It was the voice we always recognised when we were children. It was the voice we knew to avoid at all costs.

"No. Mom." Tanya took a deep breath. "This isn't any-body's fault."

"Yes it is," it was an angry whisper.

"What?"

"It's your father's fault."

"That's ridiculous. This isn't dad's fault. How can you even say that?"

"Quite easily: because it's true."

"Mom," Tanya was frustrated. "The reason Sarah's here is because she's had a complete break with reality. Granted dad's suicide probably didn't help much, but Sarah's always been a bit on the unstable side."

"She's sensitive, not unstable."

"Bloody hell," Jack said. "Do they always argue like this?"

"This is nothing," I whispered, not sure if they would hear me or not. "I only worry when they start throwing things."

"No need to whisper," Jack said walking behind them. "They can't hear a word. They're too wrapped up in their own reality to see yours."

"I know my child better than anybody. It's a mother's job to know," my mother said. "I know her faults as well as her strengths. Sarah's stubborn and it's that stubbornness that's going to get her through this."

"It's that stubbornness that got her here in the first place." Tanya always had to have the last word.

"I'm bored," Jack said. "I've heard enough from them."

"But I haven't," I said, trying to choke back tears. They did care. The knowledge of that made me stronger.

"I don't care if you have or not," Jack said.

A red curtain slid into place, cutting me off from them completely. Jack's appearance changed. He stood in the spotlight in full Freddy Mercury regalia. Music played. It was the chorus from Queen's I'm going slightly mad.

'You're missing that one final screw,' Jack sang and sounded like Freddy.

At the end of the song he pulled the microphone away from his mouth and blushed.

"I've always wanted to do that," he said.

The curtain disappeared. My mother and Tanya were gone. I was alone and listening to Jack whistle the song again.

*

Cresta was buzzing with people. Shoppers and movie-goers rushed around outside the restaurant. Teenagers on dates sat and held hands at tables around them. The music played softly in the background. Denise looked hot. Her long legs were crossed and they forced her short black dress all the way up to her crotch. She wasn't wearing any panties, which made Kevin even more excited about the evening. He knew that she would see things his way. After tonight, Carol would be out of the picture and Denise would be all his.

Denise leaned over the table towards him. Her tits tried to pop out of the low-cut dress. Things were going to go his way, he knew it.

"Whatever it is you're planning to do to Carol," Denise's voice was low and edgy, "don't."

"What are you talking about?" Kevin asked. This wasn't what he'd had in mind.

"Your plan to get rid of Carol won't work."

"How do you know that?" His mouth went dry.

"Because I won't allow you to frame her for the old man." Denise sat back and stared through him.

"I wasn't going to," he stammered.

"Carol and I are not stupid, and we're not going to turn on you."

"I know that."

"Good. Because, if you were to do something as stupid as turn on one of us, you would be very sorry."

"I'm not going to turn on you."

"That's what I want to hear." She smiled.

"But how can I be sure that you're not going to screw me over?" He lost the will to fight.

"That's easy."

"What?"

"It's simple." She smiled and tilted her head to one side. "We get married."

"What?" He didn't understand.

"We get married." She held his hand. "As your wife I can't screw you over."

"Really?"

"Really."

"So we're getting married."

"Yes."

"But, what about Carol?"

"Don't worry about your sister. I'll take care of her. She'll do what ever I say."

"Are you sure?"

"Your sister will play ball, so stop worrying."

"How can you be so sure?"

"Just trust me."

He wondered how Denise could be so sure about everything. What did she have on Carol? Could he get his hands on the info and use it to his advantage?

"Stop it," Denise said. "Stop trying to screw your sister over. It's not going to happen."

He felt her eyes looking into his soul, reading him and turning him inside out.

"What the hell?" he whispered, too afraid to put a voice to his fears.

"Relax, Kevin," she said and laughed, "You're so predictable. I read you like a book. I will always be one step ahead of you. So stop your plotting and enjoy the time you have with us or you'll be very sorry."

He didn't like threats and she would see who was one step ahead of whom. He would bide his time.

*

Carol waited for Kevin and Denise to come home from their dinner. She lay in the dark, curled up on the floor of the shower. Hot water pelted her and tears stung her eyes.

"You're a bad girl." She heard her uncle's voice. "And you know what happens to bad girls, don't you."

"They get punished," she said out loud. Her voice echoed in the darkness.

He always said the same thing before he raped her. It was her punishment for being a bad girl. She deserved to be raped. That's what he always told her.

Then one day her mother came home early. She walked into Carol's room and caught them. She didn't say anything, just turned around and left the house.

Her uncle laughed. "Even your mother thinks you deserve to be punished," he said and then he raped her again.

She tried to talk to her mother the next day, but her mother had put her hand up to silence her.

"I don't want to hear about what you and your uncle were doing. He's already told me how you begged him to do it to you and heaven only knows what possessed him to fall for your little seduction but, to save him from you and your wickedness, he'll be leaving today, after confession."

It was never mentioned again.

She couldn't help but wonder what her punishment would be now that her uncle was no longer there to punish her. Would it be eternal damnation? That had always been her mother's punishment of choice. Or would it be a slow, bloody end?

Keys rattled in the door interrupting her thoughts. She heard their voices as they came in the door.

Then she realised what her punishment was. It was Kevin. Kevin's happiness, short lived though it would be, was her punishment. But her reward would be sweet, as sweet as revenge could be.

20

Jack sat on the bed waiting patiently for me to wake up. The best way to avoid horrible thoughts is to sleep, preferably the dreamless kind. Avoidance by sleep. I was tired of dealing. The meds they were feeding me probably helped a bit. Sedatives can be wonderful.

I understood why my father pulled the trigger. If that was what he went through with Jack, I couldn't blame him for it. If I ever got out alive, my mother would have some explaining to do. That was, of course, if Jack had told the truth, which he probably hadn't.

"So do you want to hear the whole story or do you want to carry on pretending that none of this is happening?" Jack asked, leaning forward and resting his elbows on his knees.

"Do I have a choice?" I asked, not looking at him, pretending to yawn.

"Not really, no."

"Then please, don't let me stop you."

"I met your dearly departed dad a few years ago. I must say he was a stubborn old bastard. He took much longer to come around to seeing things my way than most people. You must get that from him. Anyway, your dad and I had a lot of fun together. He didn't like the idea of seeing things. At first he tried to ignore it. Rather like you've been doing lately. It's annoying. He thought if he ignored it, it would all magically disappear. Stupid humans. You all drive me crazy. You're all so goddamn predictable. But I must say, Sarah, you've surprised me. You hung in there and you do everything backwards, one of the things that's unique about you. It normally takes people a whole lot longer to work things out, that's if they ever do. They normally don't ask any questions and just kill themselves. But that's all you ever do. It's all just one question after the next with you. It makes me dizzy just listening."

"You're getting off the topic. What's the story with you and my parents?"

"Well, aren't we just the impatient one this morning." He lit a cigarette, filled his lungs with one drag and blew the smoke out slowly. The room changed. It morphed into an old-fashioned smoking room. We sat in leather wing-backed chairs, a dark wood coffee table between us. Jack put his feet up on the table.

"Where was I? Oh yes, your dad. Well … like your dad, you're a smarty-pants. He figured that something wasn't quiet right. So he played along. At times I think he was enjoying things more than I was. But my job isn't to entertain. I had to up my game. So I brought your mom into the mix."

My heart pounded an unhappy tune in my chest.

"Your mom was a lot of fun. I now know where you get your sexiness. She's all woman."

Not the way I wanted to think about my mother.

"She was also your dad's weak spot, his Achilles' heel. What can I say? Your dad was the jealous type. He couldn't handle it when I screwed your mother."

"You bastard," it came out in a whisper. I didn't want to hear anymore.

"I don't know if it was the fact that I screwed her, or that she enjoyed it, that finally drove dear old dad over the edge. After that, he did as he was told."

"Why are you doing this to us? What did my family do to deserve you?"

"There we go with the questions again. Now hush and be patient. You'll have all the answers in good time. Before he was allowed to blow his brains out he had to designate who would inherit me. He had to choose someone he cared about. It was another way to mess with his fragile little mind. He knew that the person he chose would suffer just the way he had. Three guesses who he chose? Your loving daddy decided that I should visit you and not your big sister Tanya or your dear mom. Just you. Then he blew his brains out. He was rather pathetic at the end. It was sad really." He took another drag of his cigarette. "Any questions?"

"Why?"

"Why! It's always the same story with you. Okay. It's actually quite simple. It's my job. It's also very entertaining. Granted it is boring after a few hundred years, so I'm hoping that my spotless record will earn me a promotion. A few more suicides and I'm outta here. I hear soul collectors do pretty well."

"What are you?"

"I'm a torment demon. A mid-level demon. I don't do too badly. You gotta have skills in this business."

"What happens if I don't kill myself?"

"I honestly don't know. Never had that happen before."

"Well, I guess you're about to find out. Because, no matter what you do, I'll never kill myself."

"Never is a long time, Sweetie Pie."

"I guess you just have to decide how much time and effort you're willing to invest in getting me to blow my brains out."

"What do you mean?"

"Well, wouldn't it be easier for you to simply move on, to an easier target and that way, you reach your goal a whole lot faster?"

"I hadn't thought about it that way. I must say, I prefer a challenge and, you and your dad have been that for me."

"Haven't you had enough of a challenge? Don't you want a bit of a break, a holiday?"

"A holiday?" He sounded sceptical.

"Yes, an easy target. Someone who deserves you."

"I don't know, Sarah."

"What's not to know?"

"I'll think about it. Maybe I'll get you to change your mind and then I can still move to an easier target."

"You're not going to get me to change my mind, but I'll even help you find an easy target." I was bargaining for my life with someone else's. How low could I possibly sink?

"Sweetie, you're going to have to do that anyway." He smothered his cigarette. "If you'll excuse me, I have some thinking to do."

"Wait," I screamed. "Who sent you to my father?"

He was gone in flash of smoke. My question hung in the air unanswered. It was the first time he'd exited that way. Normally he just disappeared. A dramatic departure: that was Jack, your typical demonic drama queen. Everything suddenly made sense, even if I didn't have all the answers. I knew what I had to do to survive.

*

The dinner left Kevin confused. He wasn't sure how he felt. Every time he looked at Denise he still wanted to rip off her clothes and do her then and there, but his gut feeling was to run as far away from her as he could. Then there was the part of him that wanted to strangle her pretty little neck.

But he ignored the urge. He had chosen his course and he was going to stick to it.

Carol and Denise cuddled on the couch watching some chick flick. He swallowed another gulp of beer. He was on his second refill of painkillers and the doctor wasn't going to give him another bottle. The excuse that he'd lost the first bottle had been believable but, that the second bottle had also mysteriously vanished triggered a few questions he couldn't answer. Finding a new supplier was going to be tricky. Maybe he should stick to coke? But the coke wasn't helping with the pain in his shoulder. He would have to find something stronger. Perhaps Denise's cocaine guy would have harder stuff. Maybe some heroin.

"What's wrong with you?" Carol asked, looking up at him from the couch. For a moment he thought he saw a look of disgust flash across her face, then it was gone. He didn't care what she thought of him. He didn't care what anybody thought anymore.

"My shoulder hurts," he said, rubbing the offending body part.

"Stop being such a baby," Carol said, while watching the TV.

"I'm not a baby," he said, sounding like a petulant child. "Have you told her yet?" he asked Denise, wanting to distract attention from his shoulder and the craving he felt.

"Told me what?" Carol asked, looking from Kevin to Denise and back again.

"That we're getting married," he said, enjoying the shocked

expression on Carol's face. He ignored the glare he got from Denise.

"You're what?" Carol said, staring at Denise.

"Yes, Kevin and I have decided to get married," Denise said holding Carol's hand.

"Why? When?" she stammered. "I don't understand."

"Last night," Kevin said. "Denise proposed." He enjoyed the moment.

"I see," Carol said, staring straight ahead.

"No, you don't," Denise said. "I suggested marriage to make your brother feel more secure; so that he wouldn't do anything stupid." She gave Carol a long hard look.

Denise wiped a tear from Carol's cheek. "Nothing changes," Denise said, holding Carol's face in her hands. "I promise everything is still the way it was."

Carol nodded and tried to smile.

He thought of running again but he'd come too far. He couldn't turn back.

*

"Do you think he bought it?" Carol whispered. They were hiding from Kevin. Trying to have a few minutes alone proved to be difficult. They had to wait for him to pass out from too much beer, but the coke kept him awake and hyper.

"Hook, line and sinker," Denise said. "He really thinks we're getting married."

"He's such an idiot."

"But the best will be the look on your mother's face when she arrives at the church for what she thinks is Kevin's wedding, only to discover that it's our wedding."

"And, that her precious little boy is a murdering drug addict."

They smothered their laughter.

"I can't wait," Denise said and kissed Carol with passion.

"It's going to be amazing." Carol was breathless.

21

It was long past lights out. The conversation I'd had with Jack a few hours earlier still rumbled in my head. My father killed himself to save my mother, or so he claimed, and damned me in the process. Bastard. Why hadn't Tanya been blessed with good old Jack? She was always the most stable one in the family.

Jack appeared on the bed looking composed and thoughtful.

"Firstly," he said. "No matter what happens, I'd like your permission to keep the name Jack. No one has ever named me and I like the name, so I'd like to keep it." He took a breath. "If that's okay with you?"

"Sure. No problem." I was confused. That hadn't been the opening I'd expected. "Anything else?"

"Well, I've been thinking, and I've realised that I've approached this all wrong." He looked down at his feet. "I have a tendency, just a small one, to get wrapped up in the tormenting side of the business and forget that the suicide thing is the most important part of the job. As a result, it takes me a while to close a deal. So," he took another deep breath, "um, I also sometimes forget that the greatest leading cause of suicide is depression and as much fun as I've been having tormenting you, I guess I'm going to have to depress you. So ..." Another deep breath. "If you don't mind, I would like to try one more time to get you to follow your father into the Great Beyond."

I wanted to laugh. The situation was ludicrous. He looked embarrassed, like a schoolboy explaining himself to his teacher.

"What if, after you've depressed me, I still refuse to kill myself?"

"Well, then I would find myself in new territory." He rolled his eyes. "I would have to consult with my supervisor and, trust me, that will not be fun." He sighed. "He'll then take it to the Council for a final decision."

"Fine. So can we please get on with it?" I prepared myself

for Jack's final onslaught, although I had a feeling that nothing would prepare me for what was about to come.

*

The air around us changed, it sparked. Walls disappeared and all colour drained away. Everything became grey and grainy, like an old black-and-white photo. Jack and I stood outside my cottage on my sister's property. Paint peeled off the walls. The garden was in worse condition than the one I stared at each day. The grass was dry and dead. The red roses that I'd planted outside the windows were gone and so were all the other flower beds.

"Sarah, what you're about to see is what is in store for you if you decide to live. Everything that you see here will happen. It's a forgone conclusion."

"Let's just get this over with." Seeing the state of my garden was depressing enough on its own. My stomach sank at the thought of what was waiting inside for me.

"After you." Jack opened the door and bowed, gesturing for me to go inside. The cottage was dark and cold. An acrid smell assaulted my nostrils. I remembered it being bright and cosy, just the way a home should be. But the room we stood in was not the home I remembered. It was dirty and gave me the creeps. I knew that no matter what happened to me, I would never be the same again. No music played and no birds sang outside. There was no happiness, only a total feeling of loss and desperation.

My heart pounded. I wanted to turn tail and run, but instead, I took a deep breath. I could handle whatever happened.

I saw myself sitting in the wheelchair in the middle of what had once been my lounge. My hair was unwashed and my body had wasted away. I stank. Taking a closer look at the future me, I realised that something was seriously wrong.

"If you decide to carry on, this is what will become of you," Jack said, looking at the future version of me. "You'll never walk again. Your muscles have atrophied to the point where they cannot be repaired. Your family cannot afford to pay a nurse to look after you and they cannot afford to send you to a place where you can get decent care. Rather than send you to a government institution, your sister takes you in. But we both know that your sister can't look after you. She's got the two boys keeping her busy. And your mother, well, she can't even handle being in the same room with you, let alone take care of you. So there you have it. You're going to end up alone, unable to look after yourself, sitting in your own shit because your sister can't wipe your arse for you ... and your mother doesn't care. No man will ever want you like that. You'll never have sex again, feel the warmth of a man's arms around you, or walk hand in hand with someone. You'll never have children. You're going to waste away in that chair, just waiting to die. You'll hold on for a few years, but your body will slowly give in and you'll die alone in that chair. Your body will slowly decompose while you're still trapped inside it." He smiled and took my hand.

As he spoke I watched the future me start to decompose. My body withered away into dust. A strong breeze blew through an open window, blowing my ashes away. Only the empty wheelchair remained.

"Or, you could just end it now. It'll be quick and painless. You won't have to feel the rejection of a mother who is supposed to love you. Face it, she's only showing any kind of affection at the moment because she thinks she's lost you, but the moment she thinks you're back or if she has to look after you, she'll be gone. You won't see her for dust. You don't have to go through any of this. You just have to say the word and it will all be over. What do you say? Let's just end this all, right here and now."

I clapped. He deserved a round of applause for that Oscar winning performance.

"Bravo. Really. Well done. That was a sterling performance."

"Thank you," he said, taking a low bow. "I worked hard on it."

"I could see that. The body turning to dust was a nice

touch, but I'm sorry to say that I'm not going to end it. I'm going to have to decline your offer."

"Are you nuts?" Shock registered in his voice. "Is this how you want to live?"

"No, it isn't. But there's something you've forgotten."

"What could I possibly have forgotten?"

"Me."

"What?"

"You forgot to factor me into your idea of what the future is going to be."

"That's insane. You were sitting right there."

"That was not me. That was who you want me to be. But you forgot that I'm stubborn; my mother was right about that. I won't just sit there and take it. I refuse to waste away like that. I will damn well walk again, no matter what you or some bloody doctor tells me. You also forgot my will to live. It doesn't matter how bad it is, I will find my way through it. So you can take this trumped-up idea of what my future is going to be and shove it up your arse. Because it's all bullshit, anyway." I took a deep breath and let it out slowly.

It was over.

Jack would have to let me go. I'd won. The look on Jack's face was priceless.

"And there's something else you were wrong about," I said.

"Like what?" He crossed his arms over his chest and tapped his foot.

"My mother does care and so does my sister. They would never allow that to happen to me." I smiled. "You never should have let me see them."

"That'll teach me to be nice to you," he sighed. "Well, this isn't over yet. I still have to take this higher. So don't start celebrating just yet."

*

Carol's eyes were bloodshot and puffy. Unshed tears quivered on the edge of her lashes. It warmed Kevin's heart to see her like that. Denise had added to his bliss when she'd asked Carol to be her bridesmaid and to help her plan the wedding.

She rubbed salt in his sister's wounds and he loved her all the more for it.

He couldn't have been happier. When they whispered in the corners away from him, he could now relax in the knowledge that they were planning his wedding to the woman of his dreams.

The honeymoon was going to be even better. Carol wouldn't be able to tag along. It would raise eyebrows if she did, and that was something none of them wanted. Nobody wanted any unnecessary scrutiny where their relationship was concerned. Carol would have to shut her trap and stay behind. The image of her waving, tearfully, goodbye at the airport made him smile and sigh with relief.

The wedding was in a couple of months. His parents were ecstatic. He'd never seen them that happy. He didn't want to think about how they'd react if they knew about the true relationship between the three of them. They didn't even know that their little girl was a lesbo, let alone that she liked giving her brother blowjobs. Hopefully they'd never find out. Although, if they did find out, it might kill them, then he'd inherit quite a bundle of cash.

He took a swig of beer as he watched Carol and Denise, their heads close together, looking through bridal magazines. His shoulder twinged and he thought of Sarah. He still had to deal with her, but that could wait. He was enjoying his moment of triumph. Denise and Carol were under control and he was the one holding all the cards.

When the time was right he would go and see Sarah and make her pay. He had to figure out what he would do to her, but he had time to think about that. He would savour every moment and she wouldn't know what had hit her, just like he hadn't seen the knife until she'd jabbed it into him. Stabbing her could be fun. He looked forward to seeing her. It would be an experience that neither of them would ever forget.

*

The eye drops stung, but they gave her eyes the required bloodshot and teary look.

Carol and Denise sat huddled together on the couch poring over bridal magazines. They both needed ideas for their wedding gowns. They decided that they'd both wear white.

"I keep seeing Kevin's face that night," Carol whispered, as she stared with unseeing eyes at the page of what must have been the hundredth magazine.

"Which night?" Denise asked

"The first time my uncle raped me."

"What happened that night?" Denise asked, as she took Carol's hand and squeezed it. "You never talk about it. I know that Kevin was there, but you never go into any detail about it."

"Kevin was sleeping in my room, because my mother had put Martin in Kevin's room. Kevin was sleeping on a blow-up mattress in the middle of the floor when he came in. Kevin must have woken up in the middle of it. I must have screamed or something because Martin put his hand over my mouth and Kevin stood next to the bed looking at us. He rubbed his eyes and stared at us. I was crying and in pain. I was so scared. Good old Uncle Martin told Kevin to go back to sleep. I bit Martin's hand so he'd take it off my mouth. When he did, I begged Kevin to help me, to get my parents, to do something, anything. He just looked at me and then at Martin. He turned around, went back to his bed and pulled the blanket over his head. He didn't even say anything the next morning." Carol wiped away real tears. She didn't need the eye drops to give her the required look.

"So he just went back to sleep while your uncle carried on raping you?" Denise asked, her voice thick with emotion.

"Yes. And he pretended to sleep through it every night after that while Martin lived with us."

"Bloody hell."

"Yes it was." She wiped away more tears.

"My love," Denise whispered, "I promise nobody will ever do that to you again."

"I know." She squeezed Denise's hand.

"What are you two whispering about?" Kevin asked and took another swig of his beer.

"Just wedding stuff," Denise said and smiled.

22

The sun set a few times, and I hadn't laid eyes on Jack. I stared out of the window a lot. I knew every plant by heart, even though they were mostly overgrown with weeds and dying. I even started naming them. I enjoyed naming things. Naming something made it more real. That's why I named Jack. If he was real, I wasn't crazy and, if I wasn't crazy, I could fight back.

As I waited, I tried not to think. The last thing I wanted to do was think about my father and Jack, or my mother and Jack. I didn't want to feel the pain travelling through every fibre of my being. I didn't want to feel betrayed by those who should have protected me. But I couldn't help it. All I did was think. I didn't even notice the other crazies around me. I didn't hear the screams anymore. I didn't notice the nurses or the wardens. The pain and the anger were almost unbearable but, if I could survive my father's betrayal, I could survive Jack.

I sat in my wheelchair in the darkness of my cell when Jack came back. He wasn't alone. An old man who reminded me of Gandalf stood next to him.

"So, young lady," the Gandalf look-alike said. "You've caused quite a stir in our little community. What have you got to say for yourself?"

"What can I say? I live to stir things up."

"Don't be glib, little girl. This is a serious matter." The old guy's bushy eyebrows furrowed together. "Jack, as you call him, has been doing this sort of thing for hundreds of years and has never had to come to me in all that time with this sort of problem. It's very disturbing for all of us."

"I ..." Jack tried to say something.

"Don't interrupt." The old man ran his eyes up and down the length of Jack's tall body. "I'll deal with your punishment in a moment; right now I need to deal with your mess. What possessed you to tell her the truth?"

"She ..."

"Oh, shut up. I don't want to hear your excuses. What we

need here is a solution to the problem. I guess we could kill her and make it look like a suicide. But that really wouldn't do." The old man crossed his arms and his left foot tapped rhythmically on the floor.

"Well, how about if I do eventually kill myself in a few years' time, of my own doing and without any interference from our buddy Jack, you still get the credit for it?" I asked.

"I appreciate the offer young lady, but that's not quite good enough." Gandalf looked down his long nose at me.

"She did say something about finding someone to take her place," Jack interjected.

"She has to do that anyway, so that doesn't really help now, does it? But it's all we've got; so until she finds her replacement, she stays here and you continue to torment her. Plus, should she kill herself in years to come, as she suggested, we still get something out of it. Now as for you, Jack," he said scowling. "You've got another hundred years added to your term of servitude. Should those hundred years be exemplary, you will have your promotion. Is that acceptable?"

"Yes, sir," Jack said, looking down at his shoes and clasping his hands.

"Very well, then." With that the old man disappeared, leaving me with a whole new set of questions and one big, new problem.

How was I supposed to find a replacement?

*

I sat and watched. I watched the other inmates, most were already suicidal so they probably only needed a little push. But was I really capable of sticking Jack on one of them? My survival depended on my doing just that. A girl with dirty blonde hair sat in the corner of a couch to the right of the window. She tried to hide the tell-tale scars on her wrists by pulling down the sleeves of her gown and clutching them in her small, fragile fists.

"Don't even go there," Jack whispered in my ear. "She's way too easy. I need a challenge. Something I can really sink my teeth into. I'll just have to say boo to that one and she'll be slicing into her veins."

Jack had no intention of making it easy for me: his way of getting back at me for his hundred-year extension.

There was the woman sitting on the floor and smacking her head against the wall till it bled.

"Nah. She's a total nut job. She killed her father in his sleep. Apparently the bastard had been raping her since she was six. Her brain is a complete mess. Can't do anything there. She wouldn't even notice anything weird happening." He sighed. "It's actually quite sad."

Jack was a puzzle. I didn't know from one moment to the next what he was going to do, or how he was going to react to something. His emotional side was the most surprising thing of all.

"What?" he asked. "Demons have feelings too, you know. Besides I didn't do that to her. You humans cause each other far more pain than I, or any of my kind, could ever hope to. It makes you all the more interesting and so easily corruptible."

He rejected one after the other. None of the inmates on my psyche ward measured up to Jack's prerequisites. He wanted someone who was still relatively sane, who had issues he could manipulate to drive them insane. I came to realise he didn't want anybody who was in the nut house, which included the staff. Every time I suggested one of the wardens, nurses or so-called shrinks, he rejected them out right. He didn't even bother giving an excuse. It was an immediate 'Hell, no', which left me out of options. There was no way for me to find a replacement. I was screwed, and not in a good way. If I didn't find a replacement soon, I'd be stuck in the nut house and Jack would probably end up getting me to kill myself anyway. Things were not looking good and then they got even worse.

"I should probably have pressed the issue earlier," Jack said, one morning after he rejected yet another of my suggestions. "But it has to be someone you care about, remember? That's why your daddy dearest had to pick someone in the family."

I'd tried to forget that little piece of info and hoped that

Jack would forget about it too. No such luck. How could I give Jack to someone I cared about? I'd rather keep him to myself than set him loose on anybody I loved.

*

Wedding plans were in full swing. Kevin's mother had never phoned him as much as she had over the last couple of days. There was no sign of Denise's parents. Kevin wondered if she even had any. He knew next to nothing about her, but the little he did was enough for him. Even in high school she'd been mysterious. Marrying Denise had many ups and not many downsides. If they were married she couldn't be forced to testify against him. It pissed off Carol. It made his parents happy and, it meant he got to screw her every night, for the rest of his life. There was only one fly in the ointment.

Sarah was on his mind. He couldn't stop thinking about her. Every time he looked in the mirror and saw the scar on his shoulder, every time he moved his arm he saw her face. Her blank, dead, blue eyes stared at him as she stabbed him. He had to sort her out once and for all so that he could get on with his life. The sooner the better.

He called her stupid sister and gave her some sob story about how he needed to forgive her and, that to do that, he had to see her. The sister was so frigging gullible. It must run in the family, he decided. He knew where she was. She wasn't going anywhere. The only thing was, when he did make his move, what move should he make? There were many options.

Death would be too easy for her. The gang rape option would have to wait until she got out. Then there was the knife. She'd stabbed him with her kitchen carving knife. He'd managed to bribe some cop after that farce of a trial and now, he had it. It was also the same knife he'd used to kill the old man. He could always cut off her tits or slash her face. That way no man would ever look at her or want her. He would be doing mankind a favour.

He fondled the knife he had stashed in the bedside table drawer, as he pictured slicing Sarah's face.

"When are you going to see her?" Denise stood behind him as he played with the carving knife.

"Soon," he said. Sunlight glinted off the blade.

23

The afternoon sun peeked out from between grey clouds. It had rained hard that morning. The puddles dried in the sun. I heard someone talking to one of the nurses. The voice was close by. It was familiar but I couldn't put my finger on it. It was so close.

"Looks like you've got another visitor," Jack said. "Too bad it has to be that piece of shit."

Kevin. It was Kevin's voice. He'd forgiven me, and that's why he was visiting me. My heart skipped a beat and butterflies danced in my stomach. I strained to hear the conversation he was having with the nurse.

"She used to fluctuate between a catatonic stupor and excitement. Sometimes she talks to herself and is very excited. She used to do a lot of screaming and hurt herself, which disturbed a lot of our patients. But now, she mostly just sits and stares out of the window. Lately she's been very quiet. I think the meds are starting to do their job. It takes a while to work out the correct dosage."

"I see," Kevin said.

"She also often mentions someone called Jack."

"Jack?" He sounded confused.

"Yes. Does the name mean anything to you?"

"No. I can't say that it does." He took a deep breath. "Is she able to understand what's happening around her? Can she hear me when I talk to her?"

"You have to understand, she's been through a great deal." It was the nurse's turn to pause and take a deep breath. "There was an incident with her doctor and since then she's retreated into herself even more."

"Look, just tell me if she can hear me or not. I don't care about all that other shit. I just want to know if the crazy bitch can hear me or not."

"Sir, you need to calm down. You can't upset her in any way. Do you understand me?"

"I understand. Now can I see her?"

"She's sitting right over there."

I heard his heavy footsteps make their way towards me. He hadn't forgiven me after all.

He stood in front of me. His left arm was in a sling and his hair was gelled and styled. He looked just as good as I'd remembered him, a little leaner perhaps and his skin looked a little on the grey side, but he was still as handsome as ever. He was dressed in a suit. He always looked good in a suit.

"You look like shit," he snarled down at me and then sniffed the air. "God, you stink." The thought seemed to make him happy, but then his expression changed. Anger flared in his eyes. "I have nerve damage from when you stabbed me, you frigging bitch. I'll be lucky if I ever get complete use of my arm again." He got down on his haunches. "But at least I know that you're locked away in here. My God, you really do stink." He put his fingers up to his nose to block out my stench. "You're not the hot piece of arse you used to be, that's for sure." He shook his head. "I've moved on to better things. You remember Denise and how I used to tell you that she was just my sister's friend? Well, she's been polishing my knob for quite some time now. She's so good at it that I've asked her to marry me. Today's our wedding day." He laughed. "You know, we used to laugh at you. You were so stupid. Every time you called and she was with me, she'd suck my cock while I told you some bullshit story. You bought it every time and you always begged me for more. You are so pathetic."

"I'm pathetic," I croaked out. My heart pounded its angry tune in my chest. My stomach turned to stone.

"The psycho speaks." Kevin took a step back. Surprise plastered all over his face.

"I think there's someone you should meet." My voice was hoarse. "Jack, I've found my replacement."

"I don't know," Jack said.

"What don't you know?" My throat hurt with every word I uttered. "He's everything you wanted."

"Maybe," Jack said, sounding sceptical.

"What do you mean maybe?" I was angry.

"What is going on?" Kevin turned grey.

"I guess he could be fun," Jack said.

"Of course he will be," I said. "You'll get out of here, and he's a challenge. Plus he's somebody I cared about. That fits another of your stipulations."

"That it does. I'm not so sure about the challenge part, but I'll give it a try," Jack said, making up his mind.

"Who is that?" Kevin asked. His voice quivered.

"Kevin, this is Jack. Jack, this is Kevin."

Kevin stood frozen and slowly turned from Jack to me and then back again. His mouth opened and closed like a guppy. He then turned tail and ran.

"I guess it's a good thing you didn't kill him. This way I get to party at his expense." Jack sighed. "I'm going to miss you. But, you never know. I might check in on you from time to time. So I'll see you around." Then he was gone. Jack was out of my life and I could start the long process of healing.

The picture of Jack's version of my future crept into my mind. I promised myself that I would never allow that to happen. I would recover. I would heal and I would walk again.

"Nurse," I called out. "Nurse, may I have something to drink, please?"

"Miss Van der Walt? Did you just say something?"

"Yes. May I please have something to drink?"

The nurse looked at me as though I had two heads. I realised that it was probably the first time she'd ever heard me say something coherent and of all the things I could have chosen to say, I asked for something to drink. I was thirsty and my throat hurt. All I wanted at that moment was a glass of cold water.

She scuttled off, leaving me alone, and at peace for the first time in a very long time.

*

Kevin's heart pounded. Cold sweat glistened on his skin. The man followed him out of the psychiatric hospital in Pretoria, to his car. He locked the doors and still the man managed to get in. Kevin heard laughter echo in his head as the man turned into the bloody corpse of the old homeless guy. He heard his own scream reverberate in the closed cab of his car.

"This isn't happening to me," Kevin whispered. "Not today."

He put the key in the ignition and turned the engine. Driving with one arm was a challenge.

"I love weddings," Jack said with a grin, exposing his sharp yellow teeth.

Using his right hand, Kevin put the gear shift into first and sped off, leaving rubber behind to mark where his car had been. He blocked out the sound of Jack's laughter. It wasn't real. He would make it to the chapel on time and he would make it through his wedding, without losing his mind.

Tyres screeched as he pulled into the already-full wedding venue parking area. Checking his watch, he worried that he was late, but there was still plenty of time. He got out of the car and walked towards the closed chapel doors. Jack followed him. Kevin heard another car pull in. Then a cheer erupted from inside the chapel.

The chapel doors burst open and two brides came running out.

"Oh my," Kevin's mother, Evelyn, said. "Two women getting married. Is that even legal?"

"I think so," Kevin said. "I think it's pretty cool."

"Oh my God," Evelyn whispered.

"What?" Kevin asked, looking down at his pale mother.

"Isn't that Carol?"

Jack laughed.

Kevin's stomach hit the floor and his face felt as though it was on fire.

Denise and Carol laughed as confetti was thrown over them.

*

Jack's laughter grated his last nerve. Kevin had listened to that annoying laughter all the way from the chapel to the flat he shared with the girls. He sat on the couch with a beer in his hand and a six-pack at his feet.

"You didn't see that one coming, did you?" Jack laughed.

Kevin ignored him. He didn't understand what he'd seen. Denise had married Carol, not him. They'd been planning their wedding, not his.

"Took you a while to figure that one out," Jack said and laughed again. "Your sister's right. You really are an idiot where women are concerned."

There had to be a reasonable explanation for it. There had to be.

"Oh, there is," Jack said. "They screwed you. Plain and simple. You really should have protected your little sister all those years ago. And giving Denise the shaft, for that girl Carla, also wasn't a good idea. Because you stood her up that one night, she ended up with one of your friends: a really nasty piece of work, who didn't believe in taking 'no' for an answer. You remember, don't you? He told everybody the next day what an easy lay she was. He forgot to mention that she'd said 'no' a few times and that he had to slap her around to make her submit. So because of you, both of those girls were hurt in the worst possible ways. Not that there's a nice way to be raped, but anyway."

"Shut up," Kevin yelled. "Just shut up."

"But I'm not finished," Jack said, offended. "There's so much more to tell."

"I don't want to hear it," Kevin said.

"Don't you want to know what else the girls have in store for you? Their little revenge plot goes far deeper than getting married and running off without you."

"I don't want to hear it," Kevin's voice cracked and tears ran down his face.

"But you really should." Jack smiled. "It's brilliant. Do you remember what happened to your blood-soaked T-shirt? The one you were wearing when you murdered that poor, defenceless, homeless man."

"Denise burned it."

"You sure about that?"

Kevin felt the blood drain from his face as the penny dropped and comprehension dawned.

"That's right," Jack said. "You're a bit slow on the uptake, aren't you? Good thing that it didn't work out between you and Sarah. She would eventually have realised that you were too dumb for her. Now she's a smart one, although I think Denise could give her a run for her money." Jack laughed. "Sorry," he said. "I'm getting off topic. Sarah hates it when I do that. Anyway. Where was I? Oh yes, the big revenge plan." Jack shuddered. "That T-shirt was anonymously sent to a former lover of Denise and Carol's, who happens to be a cop. Along with the bloody T-shirt was a note with your name and address. It also stated that the murder weapon could be found here and that you were the guilty murdering bastard."

Kevin watched Jack pace up and down the length of the lounge as he told the story. He tried telling himself that it was all an elaborate hoax but he knew, with a strange certainty, that every word out of Jack's mouth was the truth. Denise and Carol had done their job well.

"To be honest, I think they're being a bit unfair. You were only six years old when your uncle did the nasty with your sister, not much you could have done at the time. Plus you've had to live with being a coward all your life. That's got to suck." Jack gave him a commiserating smile. "What I don't understand is why they didn't do more to that horrible bitch of a mother? She knew what was going on and didn't do anything to save her daughter. Instead of punishing that bastard brother of hers, she punished Carol. It really doesn't make any sense to me. But Carol thought that your being a drug addict, a convicted murderer and having an incestuous relationship with your sister would bring your mother enough pain." Jack shook his head. "But I think the photos they took of you screwing your sister, and sent off to your mother today, should do the trick. What do you think?"

Kevin didn't know what to think, say or do.

"So how close are you to wanting to kill yourself? I need to know how much more work I need to put in. You see, I'm a little behind on my quota. So if you don't mind, I'd like to hurry this along."

The carving knife Sarah had stabbed him with, which he'd used on the old man, appeared in his hand.

"Come on," Jack said. "Take one for the team."

*

All Denise and Carol had to do was pack a few bags for their trip. By the time they came back, if they came back, Kevin would be behind bars. It had all worked out. Carol smiled as she unlocked the door to the flat while Denise kissed her neck. Kevin was probably waiting at the church for them. She only wished she could have seen his face.

They tumbled, laughing, through the doorway. Then Carol looked up and saw Kevin. The look on his face stopped the laughter bubbling out of her. She had never seen Kevin like that before, not even the night Martin had first raped her. His eyes were wild and panic stricken.

He sat on the couch holding the knife he'd used on the homeless man. He stared at a spot on the wall.

"You can have Carol," he said, with a strange smile

Then he took the knife, stabbed his own jugular, slicing his throat. Blood sprayed all over the room.

"Ah, man," Denise said. "Did he have to go and make such a mess?"

Carol wasn't paying much attention to the blood, or Denise.

She stared at the man with the yellow eyes standing over her brother's body. He smiled at her, exposing sharp pointed teeth.

"Hello, Sweetie," he said.

"Carol," she heard Denise say from a distance. "Are you okay?"

She couldn't answer. She couldn't move.

"I was just a little boy, Carol," Kevin said with dead eyes, blood dripping from the wound in his neck. "I was only six years old. I'm sorry I couldn't protect you. I've had to live with that. I hope you can live with what you've done to me just because I was a scared little boy, who didn't know what to do." His eyes closed and he was gone.

Carol stood alone in the darkness with the man.
"You can call me Jack," he said.

Epilogue

My mother had lost weight in my absence. She sat on the couch in her messy, over-furnished lounge. Getting out of the mental institution had taken some time. There had been a legal battle, which was a blur. After what seemed an eternity, my mother was declared my legal guardian. The first days out of the nut house had been confusing. My mother decided that I should stay with her, in my old room. She wanted me near her.

I took a deep breath and thanked my lucky stars that I was safe and on my way back to some form of normality. What was done was done and there wasn't much I could do about the past. I certainly couldn't change it. As I looked around, I realised that getting around in a wheelchair was going to be a problem. My leg muscles were taking their time to get back into the swing of things. They hadn't worked for over a year and it would take a lot of hard work to restore them to their former glory.

"Ma, you're going to have to get rid of some of this crap you've got all over the floor."

"Why?" she asked. It had probably never occurred to her that things would have to change.

"I'm still in a wheelchair, Ma. I need to be able to move around."

"Oh." She took a slow glance around the room. "I see." She looked dazed and confused as she flopped down onto the couch opposite me.

"Ma, we need to talk."

"Not today, Sweetie. You need to rest."

"No, I don't. I need some answers and you're the only one who can give them to me."

"What are you talking about?"

"Why didn't you tell me about Jack?"

"Who's Jack?"

"Don't play dumb, Ma." I took a deep breath and slowly let it go. "Jack was Daddy's demon. The one who raped you."

"Nobody raped me." She stood up and turned away from me. Her back was cold and untouchable.

"Don't lie to me, Ma. I'm not crazy." Tears made their way down my cheeks.

"I know you're not, Sweetie." Her back heaved. "I don't want to talk about this."

"We have to talk about it. I need to know that I didn't imagine it all; that this last year of hell hasn't been a complete waste. Can't you understand that?"

"Yes, I can. More than you know." Emotion distorted her voice. "I prayed that it was all in my imagination, that that night never happened." Her silence made the air thick with all the things I needed her to say. "But you need to understand that as far as I'm concerned nothing happened. It's all been a bad dream, and that's all. I can't allow it to be more than that."

"I need you to tell me what happened."

"I can't. Isn't it enough to know that you're not crazy and that I know it, too? Can't that be enough?" She turned to face me. "Can't you let it go?" Her eyes pleaded. "For both our sakes, just let it go."

"I don't think I can," I said.

"What do you want from me? Do you want me to say that something raped me? Do you want to hear how it broke your father? Do you want me to tell you how he made your father watch? Do you really want to hear all of that?"

I couldn't answer her. All I heard was the pain and anguish in her voice. Tears washed away the divide between us. I understood why she hadn't warned me. I finally understood that my mother was weak and fallible. That she was human. I understood that she couldn't face the truth of what had happened. She had protected her mind in the only way she could.

I also realised that even if she had warned me about Jack, I would have thought she was losing it, that she was the crazy one in the family. I wouldn't have listened to her and nothing would have changed. It had all happened the only way it could have. Everything was as it should be.

"Maybe we'll both be able to find some peace now that we know that what happened, truly did happen, that we didn't imagine it. Maybe now we can start to put the pieces of our lives back together," I said, trying to let her know that I understood in my own way.

"Good. Now that we've put that behind us, I've set up a weekly appointment for you with your friend Michael and you've got a physiotherapy appointment every Monday, Wednesday and Friday. We'll have you up and running in no time." She sighed. "Oh, and Kobus said the lawsuit was looking good. You'll never have to work again."

"What lawsuit?"

"We're suing the hospital for what that horrible man did to you."

"How did you find out about that?"

"One of the nurses came forward." She smiled. "Isn't that wonderful news."

"Yes," I said. "Yes, it is."

Jack's dark vision of my future turned to ashes and was replaced with my own much brighter version. I was alive, healing and would soon have a nice wad of cash thanks to the hospital and Dr. Lynche.

There was a long journey ahead of me, but I could see the light at the end of the tunnel growing brighter. I wasn't there yet, but I was getting there slowly and at my own pace.

Jack appeared behind my mother. I watched her stiffen as she felt his presence.

"I just popped in to say 'hello' to my two favourite ladies."

"We had a deal, Jack."

"I know, but I had to check in and see how things were going. And to let you know that I was right, Kevin was rather disappointing. He was too easy. No challenge whatsoever. Just as I predicted he would be, but luckily his sister is proving to be more of a challenge."

"His sister?" I asked.

"Yes. He was quite pleased by the idea that his sister would suffer. He even made me promise that I'd have her gang-raped. Was pretty insistent about it, in fact. He went out with a smile when I promised to do it."

"But they were so close." There was so much I didn't know about Kevin. "Why not Denise?"

"He and his little sister had some serious issues." Jack grinned. "I'll probably end up at Denise's door soon enough. I think she'll make a great Torment Demon or even a Vengeance Demon. That girl has got some skills. She could teach me a thing or two. But I'm hoping that Carol will put me onto her mother. That woman deserves to be tormented. I'm looking forward to getting my hands on her. Anyway I must get back to work. I have something special planned for Carol tonight. It's time to keep my promise to the dearly departed."

"Before you go," I said.

"Yes," he said with a raised eyebrow.

"Who sent you to my father?"

"That would have been your grandpa." He smiled.

"I didn't know grandpa killed himself. I thought it was a freak accident." I said, looking at my mother in shock.

"Your parents decided to make it look like an accident. Something to do with the insurance not paying out for a suicide. Clever girl." He winked at my mother, waved and then disappeared for what I hoped was the last time.

My mother and I sat across from each other in silence. We left each other to our own thoughts. We both knew that Jack would be back when he was bored. We just had to stay one step ahead of him. But until he showed up again, I had a life to live and enjoy. I also had a lot of work to do. If Jack was going to be back, I had to be ready to face him and whatever he had up his sleeve.

Gypsy jumped onto my lap and started pounding my thin, useless legs. Being able to feel her claws on my skin gave me hope. She curled up and purred herself to sleep. As I stroked her soft fur, I was at peace. At least for now.

END

About the Author

Joan De La Haye was born in Pretoria on the 17th of January 1977 at 7pm.

The youngest of three children raised by parents in the Diplomatic service, Joan was educated abroad, finally completing her education in Vienna. She speaks four languages and is qualified in clinical hypnotherapy and also has a diploma in Fine Art and Creative Design.

If you were to ask how long Joan has been writing, the answer would depend on who you asked. If you were to ask either her mother or her grandmother, they would both say that she's been writing since she first learned to hold a pencil. Joan, on the other hand, would answer that she penned her first story at the age of twelve, while sitting in her mother's office during a school holiday, to while away the time.

Joan has a profound interest in the occult and the paranormal which is evident in her writing.

You can find Joan on her blog:
http://joandelahaye.wordpress.com

Thank you for buying a Fox Spirit Book

If you enjoyed this you may enjoy our other Fox Spirit Titles:

'Weird Noir' edited by K.A.Laity

On the gritty backstreets of a crumbling city, tough dames and dangerous men trade barbs, witticisms and a few gunshots. But there's a new twist where urban decay meets the eldritch borders of another world: WEIRD NOIR.

Featuring thugs who sprout claws and fangs, gangsters with tentacles and the occasional succubus siren. The ambience is pure noir but the characters aren't just your average molls and mugs—the vamps might just be vamps. It's Patricia Highsmith meets Shirley Jackson or Dashiell Hammett filtered through H. P. Lovecraft. Mad, bad and truly dangerous to know, but irresistible all the same.

'Tales of the Nun & Dragon' collected by Adele Wearing

Come, rest your weary bones, draw a flagon and hark to the tales of Nuns & Dragons, of bravery and steadfastness in the face of mighty and implacable foes. Settle down and indulge yourself in wild flights of fancy brought to life by your fellow travellers.

The Nun & Dragon is a local like no other – share in the wild and wonderful tellings of a gifted panoply of authors, tales replete with wonder, a liberal coating of mysticism, the odd splash of darkness and a sprinkling of grim humour.

'Requiem in E Sharp' by Joan De La Haye

A troubled detective

A tormented serial murderer

Sundays in Pretoria are dangerous for selected women.

A murderer plagued by his childhood, has found a distinctive modus operandi to salve his pathological need to escape the domination of the person who was supposed to cherish him.

As The Bathroom Strangler's frenzy escalates and the body count mounts, Nico van Staaden, the lead detective on the case, finds himself confronting his own demons as he struggles to solve the murders of the seemingly unconnected victims. The lack of evidence in the sequence of deaths and pressure from his superiors are challenges he must overcome.

The resolution is bloody, savage and merciless.

Made in the USA
Charleston, SC
31 May 2013